Jack Higgins was raised in Belfast, and moved to Leeds with his mother when he was twelve years old. He left school with no qualifications and had a succession of jobs including two years as an NCO in the Royal Horse Guards serving on the East German border during the Cold War. Afterwards, he was accepted as an external student at London University and a degree in Sociology and Social Psychology took him into teaching. Before becoming a full-time author he was engaged in the training of teachers at various colleges in the West Riding and at Leeds University. He was already a leading writer of adventure stories before he wrote *The Eagle Has Landed* but this marvellously original war novel turned him into an international bestselling author. This has since been followed by a series of major worldwide successes including *Touch the Devil*, *Night of the Fox* and, most recently, *A Season in Hell*. *A Prayer for the Dying* was recently filmed with Bob Hoskins and Mickey Rourke to enormous controversy. *Confessional* has just been filmed as a four-part TV series. His work is published in more than thirty languages.

Jack Higgins
writing as Harry Patterson

The Thousand Faces of Night

Pan Books
London, Sydney and Auckland

First published by John Long 1961

This edition published 1990 by
Pan Books Ltd, Cavaye Place, London SW10 9PG

9 8 7 6 5 4

© Harry Patterson 1961

ISBN 0 330 31604 4

Typeset by Selectmove Limited, London

Printed and bound in Great Britain by
Cox & Wyman Ltd, Reading, Berkshire

for my
Mother & Father

1

They released Marlowe from Wandsworth shortly after eight o'clock on a wet September morning. When the gate was opened he hesitated for a moment before stepping outside and the man on duty gave him a push forward. 'See you again,' he observed, cynically.

'Like hell, you will,' Marlowe said over his shoulder.

He walked down towards the main road, a big, dangerous-looking man, massive shoulders swelling under the cheap raincoat they had given him. He stood on the corner watching the early morning traffic and a flurry of wind lifted cold rain into his face. On the opposite side of the road was a snack bar. For a moment he hesitated, fingering the money in his pocket, and then he took advantage of a break in the traffic and crossed over.

When he pushed open the door, a bell tinkled in the stillness. The place was deserted. He sat on one of the high stools at the counter and waited. After a few moments an old, white-haired man emerged from a door at the rear. He peered over the top of steel-rimmed spectacles and a slow smile appeared on his face. 'What would you like, son?' he said.

Marlowe's fingers tightened over the coins. For a moment he was unable to speak and then he managed to say, 'Give me twenty cigarettes.'

The old man was already reaching for them. For a brief second Marlowe looked at the packet and then he quickly opened it and took out a cigarette. A match flared in the old man's hands and Marlowe reached forward. He inhaled deeply and blew out the smoke with a great sigh. 'Christ, but I was waiting for that,' he said.

The old man chuckled sympathetically and poured strong coffee from a battered metal pot into a mug. He added milk and pushed it across. Marlowe reached for his money and the old man smiled and raised a hand. 'It's on the house.'

For a moment they looked at each other steadily and then Marlowe laughed. 'How can you tell?' he said.

The old man leaned on the counter and shrugged. 'I've kept this place for twenty years. Nearly every day during that time someone has walked down the street opposite and stood on that corner. Then they see this place and it's straight in for a packet of cigarettes.'

Marlowe grinned. 'You can't blame them can you?' He drank some of the coffee and sighed with pleasure. 'That tastes good. After five years of drinking swill I'd forgotten what good coffee was like.'

The old man nodded and said quietly. 'That's a long time. Things can change a lot in five years.'

Marlowe looked out of the window. 'You're damned right they can. I've been watching the cars. They all look different somehow. Even people's clothes look different.'

'They are different,' the old man said. 'And the people inside them are different too.'

Marlowe laughed bitterly and swallowed the rest of his coffee. 'Aren't we all?' he said. 'Everything changes. Everything.'

'More coffee?' the old man asked gently.

Marlowe shook his head and stood up. 'No, I've got to get moving.'

The old man produced a cloth and carefully wiped the counter. 'Where are you going, son? The Prisoners' Aid Society?'

Marlowe laughed briefly and a flash of genuine amusement showed in his cold grey eyes. 'Now I ask you. Do I look the sort of bloke that would apply to those people?'

The old man sighed and shook his head. 'No,' he said sadly. 'You look like a man who would never ask anybody for anything.'

Marlowe grinned and lit another cigarette. 'That's right, Dad. That way you never owe anybody anything.' He opened the door. 'Thanks for the cigarettes. I'll be seeing you.'

The old man shook his head. 'I hope not.'

Marlowe grinned again. 'Okay, Dad, I'll try to oblige.'

He closed the door behind him and began to walk along the pavement.

The rain had increased in force and bounced from the pavement in long solid rods. It soaked through the cheap raincoat within a few seconds and he cursed and hurried towards a bus shelter. The traffic had slackened down to an occasional truck or car and the pavements were deserted. As he approached the shelter a large black saloon turned into the kerb slightly ahead of him.

As he moved alongside the car a voice said, 'Hallo, Hugh. We've been waiting for you. It's been a long time.'

Marlowe stood quite still. The skin had tightened over his prominent cheekbones, but otherwise he showed no emotion. He approached the car and looked in at the man who sat behind the wheel. 'Hallo, you bastard!' he said.

A rough voice snarled from the rear seat. 'Watch it, Marlowe! You can't talk to Mr Faulkner like that.'

The man who had spoken was thick set with the coarse, battered features of a prizefighter. Next to him sat a small wiry man whose cold beady eyes were like holes in his white face.

Marlowe's gaze flickered over them contemptuously. 'The old firm. It must smell pretty high in there when you have the windows closed.'

The large man made a convulsive movement and Faulkner cried warningly, 'Butcher!' He subsided, swearing violently under his breath, and Faulkner said, 'Yes, the old firm, Hugh, and don't forget you're still a partner.'

Marlowe shook his head. 'You dissolved our partnership a long time ago.'

Faulkner frowned. 'I think not, my friend. We still have some unfinished business to settle.'

Marlowe smiled coldly. 'Five years inside has made me greedy, Faulkner. I'm not declaring a dividend this year.' He laughed harshly. 'What kind of a mug do you think I am? Go on, get out of it. And keep away from me.'

As he straightened up, the rear door started to open and a hairy paw reached out towards him. He slammed the door shut with all his force, trapping the hand so that blood spurted from beneath the fingernails. Butcher gave a cry of agony, and Marlowe leaned in the window and said, 'That's for leaving me in the lurch the night we did the Birmingham job.' He spat in Butcher's face and turned away.

He ducked into a narrow alley and began to walk rapidly along the uneven pavement. Behind him car-doors slammed and there was a heavy pounding of footsteps. He threw a hasty glance over his shoulder as the small man rounded the corner, steel glinting in his hand. Behind him lumbered Butcher, cursing freely as he wrapped a handkerchief about his right fist.

At any other time he would have turned and faced them, but not now. He had other things to do. He started running along the alley, splashing in the rain-filled gutter, his feet slipping dangerously on the greasy cobbles.

The small man gave a cry of triumph and Marlowe ground his teeth together with rage. So they thought they had him on the run, did they? They thought the years behind the high wall had made him soft. He resisted the impulse to stop running and increased his pace.

He rounded the corner at the end of the alley into a quiet street of terrace houses. For a brief moment he hesitated and then, as he started forward, he slipped and crashed to the pavement. As he scrambled to his feet a door opened and a woman stepped out with a shopping-basket on one arm. Marlowe lurched towards her and she stepped back quickly with a cry of alarm and slammed the door in his face. There came another shout from behind, and as he started to stumble painfully along the pavement a large black saloon turned into the road and came towards him.

A sudden burning anger rose inside and he clenched his fists as the car swerved into the kerb a few yards away. The rear door opened and a large, heavily built man in a brown raincoat and Homburg hat clambered out and stood, hands in pockets, waiting.

Marlowe came to a sudden halt. Behind him he could hear the sound of his pursuers' footsteps fading rapidly into the distance. The large man smiled and shook his head, white teeth gleaming beneath a clipped moustache. 'You haven't wasted any time, Marlowe.'

Marlowe grinned and walked towards him. 'I never thought the day would come when I'd be glad to see you, Masters,' he said.

'It's a day for surprises,' Masters retorted. 'I never thought I'd live to see you run from a couple of rats like Butcher and Harris.'

Marlowe scowled. 'I've got more important things to do. I can deal with those two any time.'

Masters nodded. 'I don't doubt it, but there's always Faulkner.' He took out a short pipe and began to fill it from a leather pouch. 'He saw us coming, by the way, and took off. I'm afraid Butcher and Harris are going to get very wet looking for him.' He frowned suddenly as if the idea had just occurred to him. 'Of course, you could always prefer charges.'

Marlowe grinned. 'What for? We were only having a little exercise.'

The rain increased in volume with a sudden rush, and Masters opened the rear door of the car and said, 'Let's continue this conversation in comfort at least.'

For a moment Marlowe hesitated and then he shrugged and climbed in. There was a tall young man in a fawn raincoat behind the wheel. He turned his head and said, 'Where to, Superintendent?'

Marlowe whistled. 'A super now, eh? They must be getting hard up.'

Masters ignored the thrust. 'Anywhere in particular you'd like to go?' Marlowe raised one eyebrow and took out his cigarettes. Masters smiled faintly and said to the driver, 'Just take us towards town, Cameron. My friend and I have a lot to talk over.'

Marlowe blew smoke out and leaned back. 'I've got nothing to say to you, Masters.'

Masters held a match to his pipe. After a moment he leaned back with a sigh. 'I wouldn't say that. There's a little matter of twenty thousand quid I want from you.'

Marlowe threw back his head and laughed. 'You've got

a hope.' He looked the policeman squarely in the eye. 'Listen, Masters. I was sent up for seven years. I've done five like a good little boy and now I'm out. Nobody can lay a finger on me. I'm clean as a whistle as far as the law is concerned.'

Masters shook his head. 'There's nothing very clean about you, Marlowe.'

Marlowe turned towards him, a fist raised, and the driver braked suddenly so that the car skidded a little. Masters smiled calmly. 'Keep going, Cameron. My friend isn't going to cause any trouble.'

Marlowe cursed and reached for the door handle. 'Okay, Masters. I've had enough. Stop the car and let me out.'

Masters shook his head. 'Oh, no, I haven't finished with you yet.' He puffed at his pipe reflectively for a moment. 'I've never been able to understand you, Marlowe. Not at your trial and not now. You had a normal enough background, a good education. You were even decorated in Korea, and then you came home and turned yourself into a lousy crook, a cheap hoodlum hanging round the big boys looking for easy pickings.'

Marlowe was calmer now. He said, 'I never waited around for anyone's pickings and you know it.'

'But you were driving for Faulkner and his bunch, weren't you?'

Marlowe shrugged. 'Why ask me? You seem to know all the answers.'

Masters shook his head. 'Not all of them, but I intend to.' He applied another match to his pipe and continued, 'It's just over five years since that Iron Amalgamated job was done in Birmingham. Whoever did it lifted over twenty thousand pounds, the wages for the following day. But they didn't cosh the night-watchman hard enough. He raised the alarm and the car was chased through the city. It crashed in a side street, and when a patrol car got there you were behind the wheel, half conscious. They dragged you out of the wreck clutching a black case. You wouldn't let go of it. One of the constables went to the end of the street to guide the other cars in and when he returned, his partner was laid out and you'd disappeared – with the bag, of course.'

Marlowe raised his eyebrows and yawned deliberately. 'I'm beginning to get bored. This is like seeing a film round twice.'

Masters smiled pleasantly. 'Wait a minute. It gets more interesting. You were picked up in Paddington Station next day. How the hell you managed to get clear of Birmingham I'll never know, but the important thing was that the money was gone.' He held the stem of his pipe against the side of his nose and said, 'Now I wonder where it got to?'

Marlowe shrugged. 'I said all I had to say at the trial. They proved I was driving the car. They gave me seven years, and now I'm out. So what?'

Masters nodded. 'But there's still the question of the money. You never did get around to telling us what you did with it.'

'You know, you've got a point there.' Marlowe dropped his voice a tone. 'Promise you won't let this go any further, but I gave all the money to a charity that's very near to my heart. It's a society that takes care of destitute policemen.'

'Very funny,' Masters said. 'As it happens, I prefer my own version. Faulkner pulled that Birmingham job, though we've never been able to prove it because you kept your mouth shut.'

Marlowe shrugged. 'So where does that get you?'

'To this,' Masters said. 'Faulkner pulled the job, but he never got his hands on the cash.' Marlowe started to speak but the policeman went on, 'It's no use denying it. I've got my contacts and I know he's been keeping pretty close tabs on you while you've been inside. The way I see it this is what happened. When your car crashed that night, Faulkner, Butcher and Harris were with you. You were stunned. In a blind panic, they ran for it, leaving you. Maybe they forgot the money in the heat of the moment or perhaps they left it deliberately, hoping the police would

13

think it was a one-man job. By a miracle you got away, because I picked you up myself in Paddington Station next day, but the money had disappeared.'

Marlowe stared out of the window, a frown on his face. 'What if it's all true? What if it happened exactly as you say? It still won't get you anywhere.' He laughed contemptuously. 'If you caught me with the money in my pockets you couldn't touch me. I've served my time.'

Masters sighed deeply. 'You know, I thought you were smart, Marlowe. That's what used to make you stand out amongst the crowd of mugs that hung around Faulkner's club in the old days.' He shook his head. 'Do you think you'll ever get to spend that money? Will you hell. I'm after it because to me it's part of an unfinished case. Faulkner's after it, and Butcher and Harris and every other cheap crook that knows the story. You're branded clear to the bone.'

Marlowe swung round and gripped Masters by the right arm. His face had turned to stone and there was a terrible expression in his eyes. 'Listen to me, Masters,' he said, 'and listen good. If anybody gets in my way I'll stamp him into the ground, and that goes for you, too.' His fingers dug painfully into the policeman's arm and his voice trembled slightly. 'I spent three years in a Chinese prison camp, Masters. Did you know that? I worked in a coal mine in Manchuria for twelve hours a day up to my knees in water. Most of my friends died, but I came home. And do you know what? Nobody seemed to know a war had been going on.'

'Is that supposed to be an excuse?' Masters said.

Marlowe ignored him. 'I took a job as a driver with Faulkner. Good money and no questions asked. He tried to make a monkey out of me, but I ended up making him look pretty stupid.' He released the policeman's arm. 'I've spent eight years of my life in prison, Masters, and I'm only thirty.' He leaned back suddenly. 'Okay, I've got the money. I earned it and now I'm keeping it.'

Masters shook his head slowly, and there was something like pity in his voice. 'You'll never get away with it. If

Faulkner doesn't catch up with you, I will.'

Marlowe shrugged. 'I wouldn't count on that i f I were you.'

The car slowed as they approached a junction and as the lights changed it started to pick up speed again. With a sudden movement, Marlowe jerked open the offside door, jumped out into the road, and slammed it behind him. He threaded his way quickly through heavy traffic and dodged down a side street.

Once away from people he started to run. He knew he had only a few minutes' start at the most. As he approached the end of the street he slowed and turned into another main road. A bus was pulling away from a stop in front of him, and he broke into a run and jumped on to the platform as it gathered speed.

As the bus moved away into the main traffic stream he slumped down into a corner seat. His chest was heaving and there was a slight film of sweat on his brow. He wiped it away with the back of his hand and smiled wryly. Things had moved fast, faster than he had anticipated, but he was still ahead of the game and that was all that counted.

He dropped off the bus at the next stop and went into a hardware store where he purchased a cheap screwdriver. Then he crossed the road and plunged into a maze of back-streets. He walked quickly, head lowered against the driving rain, and finally emerged into another main road where he caught a bus for the City.

A little more than an hour after giving Masters the slip he was in the vicinity of Paddington Station. It was raining harder than ever now and the streets were almost deserted. He crossed the road towards the station and turned into a narrow street that was lined on each side with tall, decaying Victorian houses.

About half-way along the street he paused and looked up at one of the houses. Above the door a grimy glass sign carried the legend 'Imperial Hotel' in faded letters. It was typical of a certain type of establishment to be found in the area. Places where a room was usually required for only an hour or two and never longer than a night. He mounted the steps slowly and passed inside.

He found himself in a narrow hall with several doors opening off it. Directly in front of him stairs that were covered with a threadbare carpet lifted to a gloomy landing. On his left a middle-aged woman was sitting in a cubicle reading a newspaper. She looked up and blinked red-rimmed watery eyes, and then carefully folded the paper. She spoke in a light, colourless voice. 'Yes, sir. What can I do for you?'

Marlowe's eyes moved quickly over the rows of keys that hung on the board behind her head. 'I'd like a room,' he said. 'Just for three or four hours.'

The woman's wet eyes flickered briefly over him. She produced a battered register and pen, and said, 'Sign here, please.'

Marlowe took the pen and hastily scrawled 'P. Simons – Bristol'. The woman examined the entry and said politely, 'Any luggage, sir?'

He shook his head. 'I've left it at the station. I'm catching a train for Scotland this afternoon. Thought I could do with some sleep while I'm waiting.'

She nodded. 'I see, sir. That will be fifteen shillings.'

He gave her a pound note and, when she turned to the board, said, 'I'll take number seven if it's vacant.' He laughed lightly. 'My lucky number.'

The woman handed him the key. 'It's facing you at the top of the stairs, sir,' she said. 'Would you like me to give you a call?'

He shook his head. 'No thanks, I'll be all right.'

He mounted the stairs quickly and stood on the landing listening. The hotel was wrapped in quiet. After a moment he unlocked the door of room seven and went in.

Light filtered palely through one dirty window, giving a touch of colour to the faded counterpane that covered the double bed. The only other furniture was an ancient mahogany wardrobe and a plain wooden chair which stood on the far side of the bed. There was a door marked 'Toilet' in one corner.

Marlowe wrinkled his nose in disgust. The room smelt musty and damp. Somehow there was an odour of corruption over everything. He went to the window and wrestled with the catch. After a moment it gave, and he lifted the sash as far as it would go and leaned out into the rain.

The hotel backed on to a maze of railway lines and he could see Paddington Station over to the left. Beneath the window a pile of coke reared against the wall, and there was an engine getting up steam not far away. He lit a cigarette and leaned out into the rain. There was a hint of fog in the air and already things were becoming misty and ill-defined. He shivered suddenly as a gust of wind lifted rain in his face, but he did not shake because of the cold. He was afraid. For one brief moment his courage deserted him and he allowed the thought to creep into his mind that perhaps the long years had been wasted. Perhaps what he had come for was no longer here.

With a sudden convulsive movement he tossed his cigarette far out into the rain and crossed to the toilet door. A small rounded oval plate had 'Toilet' printed on it in black letters, and was secured by two screws. Marlowe took out his screwdriver and started to unscrew the plate with hands that trembled slightly.

When he had taken one screw completely out, the plate swivelled and the thing which had been concealed behind it fell to the floor. He dropped to one knee and picked it up with trembling fingers. It was a small metal key. He held it in the palm of his hand, staring at it, and a sudden exultation lifted inside him. It was there. After all this time it was there.

He heard nothing and yet some instinct told him that he was not alone. He was conscious of a slight draught on one cheek and knew that the door was open. He turned slowly. Faulkner was standing just inside the door. He held up what was obviously a duplicate key to the room and twirled it gaily round one finger. 'I've got one too, old man, though nothing like as valuable as that one. What's it open, a safe-deposit box? Very clever of you.'

He came into the room followed by Butcher and Harris, who closed the door and leaned against it. Marlowe slipped the key into his pocket and said, 'How the hell did you manage to follow me?'

Faulkner sat down on the bed and fitted a cigarette into an elegant holder. 'We didn't need to, old man. You see, I knew something the police didn't. The day you were arrested I had a bit of luck. A pal of Butcher's happened to see you coming out of this place. I took the room for a couple of days, and we went over it with a fine-tooth comb. Couldn't find a thing, but I always had a hunch about it. There had to be a connection.'

Marlowe took out a cigarette and lit it carefully. 'I'm surprised at you, Faulkner,' he said. 'You must be slipping.' He looked quickly towards the two men at the door. Butcher was watching his every move, hate blazing out of his eyes. Harris had produced a flick-knife with which he was quietly cleaning his fingernails.

Faulkner said, 'Actually it was a damned ingenious hiding place, Hugh. But then you always were a cut above the average.' He smiled and leaned forward. 'Now come clean like a good chap and tell me where I can find the lock that key fits.' His smile became even more charming. 'I wouldn't try anything silly if I were you. Butcher and Harris are praying for an excuse to cut you into pieces.'

A quick fierce anger surged in Marlowe, and he grabbed Faulkner by the tie and jerked him up from the bed. 'You lousy bastard,' he said coldly. 'Do you think I'm scared of you and your third-rate toughs?'

Faulkner's eyes started from his head as he began to choke, and then Marlowe was aware of a movement to his left. He released Faulkner and turned as Harris cut viciously at his face with the knife. He warded off the blow with his right arm and was conscious of pain as the knife ripped his sleeve. He caught the small man by his left wrist and with a sudden pull, jerked him across the room to crash against the wall.

As he turned, Butcher struck at him with a heavy rubber cosh, the blow catching him across the left shoulder and

18

almost paralysing his arm. He chopped Butcher across the right forearm with the edge of his hand and the big man cried out in pain and dropped the cosh. Marlowe turned towards the door and Faulkner pushed out a foot and tripped him so that he fell heavily to the floor. Butcher moved in quickly, kicking at his ribs and face. Marlowe rolled away, avoiding most of the blows and scrambled up. Harris was back on his feet, shaking his head in a dazed fashion. He stumbled across the room and stood beside Butcher. For a moment there was a brief pause as the four men stood looking at each other and then Faulkner pulled an automatic out of his inside breast pocket.

Marlowe moved backwards until he faced them from the other side of the bed, the open window behind him. Faulkner appeared to be having difficulty with his voice. He choked several times before he managed to say, 'I'll take that key, Hugh, and you'll tell me where the money is. I don't want to use this, but I will if I have to.'

'I'll see you in hell first,' Marlowe said.

Faulkner shrugged and covered him carefully with the automatic. 'Go and get the key,' he told Butcher.

The big man started forward. Marlowe waited until he was almost on him and then he grabbed the wooden chair and tossed it straight at Faulkner. In the same moment he turned and vaulted through the open window.

He landed knee-deep in the pile of coke and lost his balance, rolling over and sliding to the bottom. He got to his feet and looked up. Butcher and Faulkner were at the window. For a moment they stared down at him and then they were pulled aside and Harris scrambled on to the windowsill. As he jumped, Marlowe turned and ran across the tracks towards some railway coaches which were standing in a nearby siding.

The fog was thickening rapidly now and visibility was poor. He stumbled across the tracks into the shelter of the coaches and paused for a moment to look back. Harris was running well and the blade of his knife gleamed dully in the rain. Marlowe started to run again. There was a terrible pain in his side where Butcher had kicked him and blood was dripping from his left arm.

As he emerged from the shelter of the coaches he saw a goods train moving slowly along a nearby track, gathering speed as it went. He lurched towards it and ran alongside, pulling at one of the sliding doors until it opened. He grabbed at the iron rail and hauled himself up.

As he leaned against the door Harris appeared, running strongly, his face white with effort. As he grabbed for the handrail, Marlowe summoned up his last reserve of strength and kicked him in the chest with all his force. The small man disappeared and then the train moved forward rapidly, clattering over the points as it travelled away from London towards the North.

For a moment longer Marlowe leaned in the opening and then he pushed the sliding door shut and slid gently down on to the straw-littered floor.

2

He lay face downwards in the straw for a long time, chest heaving as his tortured lungs fought for air. After a while he pushed himself up and sat with his back against a packing case.

The wagon was old and battered with many gaps in its slatted sides through which the light filtered. Gradually his breathing became easier and he stood up and removed his raincoat and jacket. The slash in his arm was less serious than he had imagined. A superficial cut, three or four inches long, where the tip of the knife had sliced through his sleeve. He took out his handkerchief and tied it around the wound, knotting it with his teeth.

He shivered and pulled on his jacket as wind whistled between the slats carrying a faint spray of cold rain. As he buttoned his raincoat he examined the packing cases that stood about him and was amused to find they were addressed to a firm in Birmingham. So the wheel had come full circle? He had escaped from Birmingham in a goods train five years before. Now he was on his way back again. Masters would have been amused.

He sat down with his back against a packing case by the door and wondered what Masters was doing now. Probably making sure that every copper in London had his description. Faulkner would be doing exactly the same thing, in his own way. Marlowe frowned and fumbled for a cigarette. London was out of the question for the moment. With every crook in town on the watch for him, he wouldn't last half an hour.

He thrust his hands deep into his pockets and considered the position. Perhaps things had worked out the best after all. A week or two in the Midlands or the North to let things cool off and then he could return quietly and collect what he had left in the safe deposit of the firm near Bond Street.

His fingers fastened over the key in his jacket pocket and he took it out and examined it. Twenty thousand pounds. He smiled suddenly. He had waited for five years. He could afford to wait for another week or two. He replaced the key in his pocket, pulled his cap down over his eyes, and went to sleep.

He came awake slowly and lay in the straw for a moment trying to decide where he was. After a while he remembered and struggled to his feet. He was cold and there was a dull, aching pain in his side where Butcher had kicked him. The train was moving fast, rocking slightly on the curves, and when he pulled the door open a gust of wind dashed violently into his face.

A curtain of fog shrouded the fields, cutting visibility down to thirty or forty yards. The cold air made him feel better and he sat down again, leaving the door open, and considered his next move.

Birmingham was out. There was always the chance that Faulkner might have discovered the train's destination. There could easily be a reception committee waiting.

Faulkner had friends everywhere. It would be best to leave the train at some small town farther along the line. The sort of place that had a name no one had ever heard of.

He emptied his pockets and checked on his available assets. There was an insurance card, his driving licence which he had renewed each year he had been in prison, and fifteen shillings in silver. He still had ten cigarettes left in the packet he had bought in the snack bar. He smiled ruefully and decided it was a good job he had the licence. With luck he might be able to get some sort of a driving job. Something that would keep him going until he was ready to return to London.

The train began to slow down and he got up quickly and closed the door leaving a narrow gap through which he could stare out into the fog. A signal box loomed out of the gloom and a moment later, the train moved past a small station platform. Marlowe just had time to make out the name Litton before the station was swallowed up by the fog.

He shrugged and a half-smile appeared on his face. This place sounded as good as any. He pushed open the door and as the train slowed even more, he dropped down into the ditch at the side of the track. Before him there was a thorn hedge. He moved along it for a few yards until he found a suitable gap through which he forced his way into a quiet road beyond. The rain was hammering down through the fog unmercifully and he pulled up his coat collar and began to walk briskly along the road.

When he came to the station he paused and examined the railway map that hung on the wall in a glass case. He had little difficulty in finding Litton. It was on the main line, about eighty miles from Birmingham. The nearest place of any size was a town called Barford, twelve or fifteen miles away.

The hands of the clock above the station entrance pointed to three and he frowned and started down the hill towards the village, dimly seen through the fog. He had obviously slept on the train for longer than he had imagined.

The main street seemed to be deserted and the fog was much thicker than it had been on the hill. He saw no one as he walked along the wet pavement. When he paused for a moment outside a draper's shop his reflection stared out at him from a mirror in the back of the window. With his cap pulled down over his eyes and his great shoulders straining out of the sodden raincoat, he presented a formidable and menacing figure.

He lifted his left hand to wipe away the rain from his face and cursed softly. Blood was trickling down his arm, soaking the sleeve of his raincoat. He thrust his hand deep into his pocket and hurried on. He had to find somewhere quiet where he could fix that slash before he ran into anyone.

The street seemed to be endless. He had been walking for a good ten minutes before he came to a low stone wall topped by spiked railings. A little farther along there was an open iron gate and a sign which read Church of the Immaculate Heart, with the times of Mass and Confession in faded gold letters beneath it.

He walked along the flagged path and mounted the four or five steps that led to the porch. For a moment he hesitated and then he pulled off his cap and went inside.

It was warm in there and very quiet. For a little while he stood listening intently and then he slumped down in a pew at the back of the church. He looked down towards the winking candles and the altar and suddenly it seemed to grow darker and he leaned forward and rested his head against a stone pillar. He was more tired than he had been in a long time.

After a while he felt better and stood up to remove his raincoat and jacket. The handkerchief had slipped down his arm exposing the wound and blood oozed sluggishly through the torn sleeve of his shirt. As he started to fumble with the knotted handkerchief there was a slight movement at his side. A voice said quietly, 'Are you all right? Can I help you?'

23

He swung round with a stifled exclamation. A young woman was standing beside him. She was wearing a man's raincoat that was too big for her and a scarf covered her head. 'How the hell did you get there?' Marlowe demanded.

She smiled slightly and sat down beside him. 'I was sitting in the corner. You didn't notice me.'

'I didn't think anyone would be in church in the middle of the afternoon,' he said. 'I came in out of the rain to fix my arm. The bandage has slipped.'

She lifted his arm and said calmly, 'That looks pretty nasty. You need a doctor.'

He jerked away from her and started to untie the handkerchief with his right hand. 'It's only a bad cut,' he said. 'Doesn't even need stitching.'

She reached over and gently unfastened the knot. She folded the handkerchief into a strip and bound it tightly about the wound. As she tied it she said, 'This won't last for long. You need a proper bandage.'

'It'll be all right,' Marlowe said. He stood up and pulled on his coat. He wanted to get away before she started asking too many questions.

As he belted his raincoat she said, 'How did you do it?'

He shrugged. 'I've been hitch-hiking from London. Going to Birmingham to look for work. I ripped myself open on a steel spike when I was climbing down from a lorry.'

He started to walk away and she followed at his heels. At the door, she kneeled and crossed herself and then she followed him out into the porch.

'Well, I'd better be off,' Marlowe said.

She looked out into the driving rain and the fog and said, with a slight smile, 'You won't stand much chance of a lift in this.'

He nodded and said smoothly, 'If I can't, I'll catch a bus to Barford. I'll be all right.'

'But there isn't a bus until five,' she said. 'It's a limited service on this road.' She appeared to hesitate and then

24

went on, 'You can come home with me if you like. I'll bandage that cut for you properly. You've plenty of time to spare before the bus goes.'

Marlowe shook his head and moved towards the top step. 'I wouldn't dream of it.'

Her mouth trembled and there was suppressed laughter in her voice as she replied, 'My father should be home by now. It will be all quite proper.'

An involuntary smile came to Marlowe's face and he turned towards her. For the first time he realized that she had a slight foreign intonation to her speech and an oddly old-fashioned turn of phrase. Suddenly and for some completely inexplicable reason, he felt completely at home with her. He grinned and took out his cigarettes. 'You're not English, are you?'

She smiled back at him, at the same time refusing a cigarette with a slight gesture of one hand. 'No, Portuguese. How did you know? I rather prided myself on my accent.'

He hastened to reassure her. 'It isn't so much your accent. For one thing, you don't look English.'

Her smile widened. 'I don't know how you intended that, but I shall take it as a compliment. My name is Maria Magellan.'

She held out her hand. He hesitated for a moment and then took it in his. 'Hugh Marlowe.'

'So! Now we know each other and it is all very respectable,' she said briskly. 'Shall we go?'

He paused for only a moment before following her down the steps. As she passed through the gate in front of him he noticed that she was small, with the ripe figure peculiar to southern women and hips that were too large by English standards.

They walked along the pavement, side by side, and he glanced covertly at her. Her face was smoothly rounded with a flawless cream complexion. The eyebrows and the hair that escaped from under the scarf were coal black and her red lips had an extra fullness that suggested sensuality.

25

She turned her head unexpectedly at one point and caught him looking at her. She smiled. 'You're a pretty big man, Mr Marlowe. How tall are you?'

Marlowe shrugged. 'I'm not sure. Around six-three, I think.'

She nodded, her eyes travelling over his massive frame. 'What kind of work are you looking for?'

He shrugged. 'Anything I can get, but driving is what I do best.'

There was a gleam of interest in her eyes. 'What kind of driving?'

'Any kind,' he said. 'Anything on wheels. I've driven the lot, from light vans to tank-transporters.'

'So! You were in the Army?' she said and her interest seemed to become even more pronounced.

Marlowe flicked his cigarette into the rain-filled gutter. 'Yes, I think you could say I was in the Army,' he said and there was a deadness in his voice.

She seemed to sense the change of mood and lapsed into silence. Marlowe walked moodily along beside her trying to think of something to say, but it was not necessary. They turned into a narrow lane and came to a five-barred gate which was standing open. She paused and said, 'Here we are.'

A gravel drive disappeared into the fog in front of them and Marlowe could make out the dim shape of a house. 'It looks like a pretty big place,' he said.

She nodded. 'It used to be a farmhouse. Now there's just a few acres of land. We run it as a market garden and fruit farm.'

He looked up into the rain. 'This kind of weather won't be doing you much good.'

She laughed. 'We haven't done too badly. We got nearly all the apples in last week and most of our other produce is under glass.'

A gust of wind lifted across the farmyard, rolling the fog in front of it, and exposed the house. It was an old, grey stone building, firmly rooted into the ground and weathered by the years. On one side of the yard there were several outbuildings and on the other, a large, red-roofed barn.

The front door was protected by an old-fashioned glass porch and outside it a small yellow van was parked. INTER-ALLIED TRADING CORPORATION – BARFORD, was printed on its side in neat black letters. Maria Magellan paused abruptly and there was something like fear on her face. She darted forward and entered the house.

Marlowe followed more slowly. He ducked slightly under the low lintel of the door and found himself in a wide, stone-flagged hall. The girl was standing outside a door on the left through which angry voices could be heard. She flung the door open and entered the room and Marlowe waited in the hall, hands thrust deep into his pockets, and watched.

Inside the room two men faced each other across a table. One of them was old with grizzled hair and a white moustache that stood out clearly against swarthy skin that was the colour of tanned leather.

The other was a much younger man, powerfully built with good shoulders. His face was twisted menacingly as he said, 'Listen you old fool. Either you come in with us or you go out of business. That's Mr O'Connor's last word.'

The old man's eyes darted fire and he slammed a hand hard against the table. His English was good but with a heavy accent and his voice was trembling with rage. 'Listen, Kennedy. You tell O'Connor this from me. Before he puts me out of business I put a knife into him. On my life I promise it.'

Kennedy laughed contemptuously. 'You bloody old fool,' he said. 'Mr O'Connor can stamp you into the dirt any time he wants. You're small stuff, Magellan.'

The old man gave a roar of anger and moved fast around the table. He swung hard with his right fist, but the years were against him. Kennedy blocked the punch with ease. He grabbed the old man by the shirt and started to beat him across the face with the flat of his hand. The girl screamed and ran forward, tearing at Kennedy with her fingers. He pushed her away with such force that she staggered across the room and lost her balance.

A cold rage flared in Marlowe and he moved forward into the room. Kennedy raised his hand to strike the old man again and Marlowe grabbed him by the shoulder and swung him round so that they faced each other. 'How about trying me?' he said. 'I'm a bit nearer your size.'

Kennedy opened his mouth to speak and Marlowe smashed a fist into it. The tremendous force of the blow hurled Kennedy across the table. He gave a terrible groan and pulled himself up from the floor. Marlowe moved quickly around the table and grabbed him by the front of his jacket. 'You bastard!' he said. 'You dirty, lousy bastard.'

And then a mist came before his eyes and it wasn't Kennedy's face that he saw before him. It was another face. One that he hated with all his being and he began to beat Kennedy methodically, backwards and forwards across the face, with his right hand.

The girl screamed again, high and clear, 'No, Marlowe! No – you'll kill him!'

She was tugging at his arm, pleading frantically with him, and Marlowe stopped. He stood for a moment staring stupidly at Kennedy, fist raised, and then he gently pushed him back against the table.

He was trembling slightly and there was still that slight haze before his eyes, almost as if some of the fog had got into the room. He clenched his fists to try and steady the trembling and noticed that blood was trickling down his left sleeve again.

The girl released her hold on him. 'I'm sorry,' she said. 'I had to stop you. You would have killed him.'

Marlowe nodded slowly and passed a hand across his face. 'You did right. Sometimes I don't know when to stop and this rat isn't worth hanging for.'

He moved suddenly and grabbing Kennedy by the collar, propelled him roughly out of the room and into the hall. He pushed him through the porch and flung him against the van. 'If you've got any sense you'll get out of here while you've got a whole skin,' he said. 'I'll give you just five minutes to gather your wits.'

Kennedy was already fumbling for the handle of the van door as Marlowe turned and went back into the house.

3

When he went into the room there was no sign of Maria, but her father was busy at the sideboard with a bottle and a couple of glasses. His face split into a wide grin and he walked quickly across and handed Marlowe a glass. 'Brandy – the best in the house. I feel like a young man again.'

Marlowe swallowed the brandy gratefully and nodded towards the window as the engine of the van roared into life. 'That's the last you'll see of him.'

The old man shrugged and an ugly look came into his eyes. 'Who knows? Next time I'll be prepared. I'll stick a knife into his belly and argue afterwards.'

Maria came into the room, a basin of hot water in one hand and bandages and a towel in the other. She still looked white and shaken, but she managed a smile as she set the bowl down on the table. 'I'll have a look at that arm now,' she said.

Marlowe removed his raincoat and jacket and she gently sponged away congealed blood and pursed her lips. 'It doesn't look too good.' She shook her head and turned to her father. 'What do you think, Papa?'

Papa Magellan looked carefully at the wound and a sudden light flickered in his eyes. 'Pretty nasty. How did you say you got it, boy?'

Marlowe shrugged. 'Ripped it on a spike getting off a truck. I've been hitching my way from London.'

29

The old man nodded. 'A spike, eh?' A light smile touched his mouth. 'I don't think we need bother the doctor, Maria. Clean it up and bandage it well. It'll be fine inside a week.'

Maria still looked dubious and Marlowe said, 'He's right. You women make a fuss about every little scratch.' He laughed and fished for a cigarette with his right hand. 'I walked a hundred and fifty miles in Korea with a bullet in my thigh. I had to. There was no one available to take it out.'

She scowled and quick fury danced in her eyes. 'All right. We don't get the doctor. Have it your own way. I hope your arm poisons and falls off.'

He chuckled and she bent her head and went to work. Papa Magellan said, 'You were in Korea?' Marlowe nodded and the old man went over to the sideboard and came back with a framed photo. 'My son, Pedro,' he said.

The boy smiled stiffly out of the photo, proud and self-conscious of the new uniform. It was the sort of picture every recruit has taken during his first few weeks of basic training. 'He looks like a good boy,' Marlowe remarked in a non-committal voice.

Papa Magellan nodded vigorously. 'He was a fine boy. He was going to go to Agricultural College. Always wanted to be a farmer.' The old man sighed heavily. 'He was killed in a patrol action near the Imjin River in 1953.'

Marlowe examined the photo again and wondered if Pedro Magellan had been smiling like that when the bullets smashed into him. But it was no use thinking about that because men in war died in so many different ways. Sometimes quickly, sometimes slowly, but always scared, with fear biting into their faces.

He grunted and handed back the photograph. 'That was a little after my time. I was captured in the early days when the Chinese took a hand.'

Maria looked up quickly. 'How long were you a prisoner?'

'About three years,' Marlowe told her.

The old man whistled softly. 'Holy Mother, that's a long

time. You must have had it rough. I hear those Chinese camps were pretty tough.'

Marlowe shrugged. 'I wouldn't know. I wasn't in a camp. They put me to work in a coal mine in Manchuria.'

Magellan's eyes narrowed and all humour left his face. 'I've heard a little about those places also.' There was a short silence and then he grinned and clapped Marlowe on the shoulder. 'Still, all this is in the past. Maybe it's a good thing for a man, like going through fire. A sort of purification.'

Marlowe laughed harshly: 'That sort of purification I can do without.'

As Maria pressed plaster over the loose ends of the bandage she said quietly, 'Papa has had a little of that kind of fire in his time. He was in the International Brigade in Spain. The Fascists held him in prison for two years.'

The old man shrugged expressively and raised a hand in protest. 'Why speak of these things? They are dead. Ancient history. We are living in the present. Life is often unpleasant and always unfair. A wise man puts it all down to experience and does the best he can.'

He stood, hands in pockets, smiling at them and Maria said, 'There, it is finished.'

Marlowe stood up and began to turn down the tattered remnants of his shirt sleeve. 'I'd better be going,' he said. 'What time did you say that bus left?'

A frown replaced the smile on Magellan's face. 'Going? Where are you going?'

'Birmingham,' Marlowe told him. 'I'm hoping to get a job there.'

'So you go to Birmingham tomorrow,' the old man said. 'Tonight you stay here. In such weather to refuse shelter to a dog would be a crime. What kind of a man do you think I am? You appear from the fog, save me from a beating, and then expect me to let you disappear just like that?' He snorted. 'Maria, run a hot bath for him and I will see if I can find a clean shirt.'

Marlowe hesitated. Every instinct told him to go. To leave now before he became further involved with these

31

people; and he looked at Maria. She smiled and shook her head. 'It's no use, Mr Marlowe. When Papa decides on something the only thing to do is agree. It saves time in the long run.'

He looked out of the window at the gloom outside and thought about that bath and a meal and made his decision. 'I give in,' he said. 'Unconditional surrender.'

She smiled and went out of the room. The old man produced a briar pipe and filled it from a worn leather pouch. 'Maria told me a little about you when you were outside with Kennedy,' he said. 'She tells me you're a truck driver.'

Marlowe shrugged. 'I have been.'

Magellan puffed patiently at his pipe until it was drawing properly. 'That slash on your arm,' he said. 'How did you say you got it?'

'From a broken hook in the tailboard of a truck,' Marlowe told him. 'Why?'

The old man shrugged. 'Oh, nothing,' he said carefully, 'except that I had a very active youth and I know a knife wound when I see one.'

Marlowe stiffened, anger moving inside him. He clenched a fist and took a step forward and the old man produced a battered silver cigarette case and flicked it open. 'Have a cigarette, son,' he said calmly. 'They soothe the nerves.'

Marlowe sighed deeply and unclenched his fist. 'Your eyes are too good, Papa. One of these days they're going to get you into trouble.'

The old man shrugged. 'I've been in trouble before.' He held out a match in cupped hands. 'How about you, son?'

Marlowe looked into the wise, humorous face and liked what he saw. 'Nothing I couldn't handle, Papa.'

The old man's eyes roved briefly over his massive frame. 'I can imagine. It would take a good man to put you down, but there's another kind of trouble that isn't so easy to handle.'

Marlowe raised an eyebrow. 'The law?' He smiled and shook his head. 'Don't worry, Papa. They won't come knocking at your door tonight.' He raised his arm. 'I can explain this. I was asleep in the back of a truck. Woke up to find some bloke going through my pockets. He pulled a knife and ripped my sleeve. I smacked his jaw and dropped off the truck. That's how I arrived here.'

Magellan threw back his head and laughed. 'Heh, I bet that fella doesn't wake up till the truck gets to Newcastle.'

Marlowe sat down in a chair and laughed with him. He felt easier now and safer. 'It's a good job we were near here,' he said. 'I didn't even know Litton was on the map.'

Magellan nodded. 'It's a quiet little place. Only seven or eight hundred people live around here.'

Marlowe grinned. 'Seems to me it's getting pretty lively for a quiet little place. What about the character I tossed out on his ear?'

The old man frowned. 'Kennedy? He was working for me until a few days ago as a driver. Now he's with Inter-Allied Trading.'

Marlowe nodded. 'I noticed the fancy yellow van when I came in. Who's this bloke O'Connor? The big boss?'

The old man snorted and fire glinted in his eyes. 'He likes to think he is, but I remember him when he was small. Very small. He had an old truck and did general haulage work. The war was the making of him. He wasn't too fussy about what he carried and always seemed to be able to get plenty of petrol when other people couldn't. Now he has twenty or thirty trucks.'

'And doesn't like competition,' Marlowe said. 'What's he trying to do? Put you out of business?'

'He offered to buy me out, but I told him I wasn't interested. The smallholding on its own isn't enough to give us a good living. I have three Bedford trucks as well. Once a month we deliver coal round the village and the outlying farms. The rest of the time we do general haulage work. I've formed a little co-operative between seven or eight market gardeners near here. They're all in a pretty small way. Together we can make it pay by using my trucks for transportation and selling in bulk.'

Marlowe was beginning to get interested. 'Even so, there can't be a fortune in that, Papa,' he said. 'What's O'Connor after?'

The old man hastened to explain. 'It isn't the haulage work he's interested in. It's the produce itself. You see about eighteen months ago he took over a large fruit-and-vegetable wholesalers in Barford Market. Since then he's bought out another and purchased a controlling interest in two more. Now he virtually controls prices. If you want to sell, you sell through him.'

Marlowe whistled softly. 'Very neat, and legal too. What's he got against you?'

The old man shrugged. 'He doesn't like my little co-operative. He prefers to deal with all the small men individually. That way he can get the stuff at rock-bottom prices and re-sell in Birmingham and other large cities at an enormous profit.'

'Hasn't anybody tried to stand up to him?' Marlowe asked.

Magellan nodded. 'Naturally, but O'Connor is a powerful man and Barford is a very small town. He can exert influence in many ways. Besides his more subtle methods there are others. A gang of young hooligans started a fight the other day in the crowded market and a stall was wrecked in the process. Of course, O'Connor knew nothing about it, but the stallholder now toes the line.'

'What about Kennedy?' Marlowe said. 'Where does he fit in?'

The old man's face darkened. 'He worked for me for nearly six months. I never liked him, but good drivers are scarce in a place like this. One day last week he told me he was leaving. I offered him a little more money if he would stay, but he laughed in my face. Said he could double it working for O'Connor.' He sighed deeply. 'I think O'Connor is beginning to think he's God in these parts. It's difficult to know what to do.'

'I suppose it hasn't occurred to anybody to kick his bloody teeth in,' Marlowe said.

Papa Magellan smiled softly. 'Oh, yes, my friend. Even

that has passed through my mind, but O'Connor's business has many ramifications these days. He has imported some peculiar individuals to work for him. Anything but country-bred.'

'Sounds interesting,' Marlowe said, 'but even that kind can be handled.' He stood up and stretched, and walked a few paces across the room. 'How are you going to fight him?'

Magellan smiled. 'I've already started. My other driver is a young fellow called Bill Johnson, who lives in the village. O'Connor offered him a good job at better money. Bill told him to go to hell. I've sent him into Barford today with a truck-load of fruit and vegetables. He's making the rounds of all the retail shops, offering to sell to them direct.'

'And you think that will work?'

Magellan shrugged. 'I don't see why not. Even O'Connor can't control everybody. He certainly can't intimidate every shopkeeper in Barford and district.'

Marlowe shook his head slowly. 'I don't know, Papa. It's a little too simple.'

The old man jumped up impatiently. 'It's got to work. He isn't God. He can't control everybody.'

'He can have a damn good try,' Marlowe said.

For a moment it seemed as if Magellan was going to explode with anger. He glared, eyes flashing, and then turned abruptly and went over to the fireplace. He stood looking down into the flames, shoulders heaving with suppressed passion, and Marlowe helped himself to another brandy.

After a while the old man spoke without turning round. 'It's a funny world. After the Spanish war when I returned home to Portugal, I found I was an embarrassment to the government. Franco was able to touch me even there. So I came to England. Now, after all these years, I find he can still touch me. Franco – O'Connor. There isn't any difference. It's the same pattern.'

'You're learning, Papa,' Marlowe said. 'It's the same problem, and the solution is always the same. You've got

35

to fight. If he uses force, use more force. If he starts playing it dirty, then you've got to play it dirtier.'

'But that's horrible. We aren't living in a jungle.' Maria had come quietly back into the room and spoke from just inside the door.

Marlowe raised his glass to her and grinned cynically. 'It's life. You either survive or go under.'

Papa Magellan had turned to face them. For a moment he looked searchingly at Marlowe, and then he said, 'That job you're looking for. Why go to Birmingham? You can have one right here working in Kennedy's place.'

Marlowe swallowed the rest of his brandy and considered the idea. It was just what he was looking for. A job in a quiet country town where nobody knew him. He could lie low for a few weeks, and then return to London to pick up the money when all the fuss had died down. After that, Ireland. There were ways and means if you knew the right people.

The whole idea sounded very attractive, but there was the added complication of the trouble with O'Connor. If that got too messy the police would step in. Contact with the police was the last thing he wanted at the moment.

He put down his glass carefully. 'I don't know, Papa. I'd have to think it over.'

'What's the matter? Are you afraid?' Maria said bitingly.

Her father waved a hand at her impatiently. 'You could stay here, son. You could have Pedro's old room.'

For several moments there was a silence while they waited for him to answer. The old man was trembling with eagerness, but the girl seemed quiet and withdrawn. Marlowe looked at her steadily for several moments, but she gave no sign of what she hoped his decision would be. As he looked at her she blushed and frowned slightly, and he knew that she didn't like him.

He half smiled and turned back to the old man. 'Sorry, Papa. I'm all for a quiet life, and it sounds to me as if you're in for quite a party in the near future.'

Magellan's face crumpled in disappointment and his shoulders sagged. All at once he was an old man again.

A very old man. 'Sure, I understand, son,' he said. 'It's a lot to ask a man.'

Maria moved over beside him quickly and slipped a hand round his shoulders. 'Don't worry, Papa. We'll manage.' She smiled proudly at Marlowe. 'My father had no right to ask you, Mr Marlowe. This is our quarrel. We can look after ourselves.'

Marlowe forced a smile to hide the quick fury that moved inside him. He was seething with anger, and mostly it was against himself. For the first time in years he felt ashamed. 'We can look after ourselves,' she said. An old man, a young girl. He wondered just how long they would last when O'Connor's tough boys moved in and really cracked down on them.

He reached for his coat and kept his face steady. Whatever happened he wasn't going to get involved. All he had to do was keep his nose clean and lie low for a couple of weeks and there was a fortune waiting for him. A man would be a fool to risk everything after five years of blood and sweat. And for what? For an old man and a girl he'd known for precisely an hour.

He buttoned his coat and said, 'Maybe I'd better be leaving after all.'

Before Magellan could reply there was the sound of a truck turning into the yard outside. It halted at the door and the engine died. 'It must be Bill,' Maria said, and there was excitement in her voice. 'I wonder if he's had any luck?'

The outside door rattled and steps dragged along the corridor. A figure appeared in the doorway and stood there, swaying slightly. He was a young man of medium size wearing a leather jacket and corduroy cap. His fleshy, good-natured face was drawn and white with pain. One of his eyes was disfigured by a livid bruise, and his mouth was badly swollen, with blood caking a nasty gash in one cheek.

'Bill!' Maria said in a horrified voice. 'What is it? What have they done to you?'

Johnson moved forward unsteadily and sank down into a chair while Papa Magellan quickly poured brandy into

37

a glass and handed it to him. Marlowe stood in the background quietly watching.

'Who beat you up, boy?' Magellan demanded grimly. 'O'Connor's men?'

Johnson swallowed his brandy and gulped. He appeared to find difficulty in speaking. Finally he said, 'Yes, it was that big chap, Blackie Monaghan. I went round the shops like you told me, and it worked fine. I got rid of all the stuff for cash.' He pulled a bundle of banknotes out of his jacket pocket and tossed them on to the table. 'One or two people told me they weren't interested. I think someone must have tipped O'Connor off.'

He paused again and closed his eyes as if he was on the point of passing out. Marlowe had been watching him closely. A cynical grin curled the corners of his mouth. Johnson had been slapped around a little, but nothing like as badly as he was trying to make out. He was over-dramatizing the whole thing, and there had to be a reason.

'Go on, son,' Magellan said sympathetically. 'Tell us what happened then.'

'I was having a cup of tea in the transport café just this side of Barford on the Birmingham road. Monaghan came in with a couple of young toughs that hang around with him. They always turn up at the Plaza on Saturday nights after the pubs close, causing trouble. Monaghan followed me outside and picked a fight. Said I'd been messing around with his girl at the dance last Saturday night.'

'Is that true?' Magellan asked.

Johnson shook his head. 'I didn't even know what he was talking about. I tried to argue with him, but he knocked me down. One of his friends kicked me in the face, but Monaghan stopped him and said I'd had enough. He told me I'd stay out of Barford if I knew what was good for me.'

Magellan shook his head in bewilderment. 'Why this?' he said. 'I don't understand?'

Marlowe laughed shortly. 'It's the old tactics, Papa. Officially this has nothing to do with O'Connor's feud

38

with you. It's just a coincidence that Johnson works for you.'

Maria's face was white with anger. 'We must go to the police,' she said. 'He can't get away with this.'

Marlowe shrugged. 'Why not? If Johnson went to the police what good would it do? It wouldn't touch O'Connor. Monaghan would be fined a couple of pounds for common assault and that would be that.'

'I don't want to go to the police,' Johnson interrupted, and there was alarm in his voice.

Papa Magellan frowned. 'Why not, son? You could have the satisfaction of seeing Monaghan in court, at least.'

Johnson got up. All at once he seemed capable of standing without swaying. His voice was a little shrill as he said, 'I don't want any more trouble. I don't want to get mixed up in this any further. I didn't know it was going to be like this.' His face was stained with fear, and there was a crack in his voice. 'I'm sorry, Mr Magellan. You've been pretty good to me, but I'll have to look for another job.' He stood there, twisting the cap between his hands. 'I won't be in tomorrow.'

There was a moment of shocked silence, and Maria turned away, stifling a sob. Magellan reached out blindly for support, his whole body sagging so that he looked on the point of collapse.

Marlowe found himself reaching for the old man, supporting him with his strong arms, easing him down into a chair. 'Don't worry, Papa,' he said. 'It's going to be all right. Everything's going to be fine.'

He straightened up and looked at Johnson. Shame was beginning to replace the look of fear on the other's face, and then that terrible, uncontrollable anger that he was powerless to control, lifted inside Marlowe. He surged forward and grabbed Johnson by the throat and shook him like a rat. 'You dirty, yellow little swine,' he raged. 'I'll give you something you really will remember.'

He flung Johnson out into the hall with all his force. The man lost his balance and fell to the floor. As Marlowe advanced towards him he scrambled to his feet gibbering with fear, and then Maria grabbed at Marlowe's hair, wrenching back his head. She slapped him across the face and screamed, 'Stop it! Hasn't there been enough of this for one day?'

As Marlowe raised an arm to brush her away, Papa Magellan ducked through the door, suddenly active, and clutching Johnson by the shoulder pushed him towards the outside door. 'Go on, get out of here for God's sake!' he said. Johnson threw one terrified look over his shoulder and scrambled through the door and out into the fog.

There was quiet except for Marlowe's heavy breathing. Maria was not crying this time. Her face was flushed and her eyes were flashing. 'What is wrong with you?' she demanded fiercely. 'Do you want to hang some day? Can't you control yourself? Is your answer to everything violence?'

Marlowe stirred and looked down at her. He swallowed hard and said, 'When I was a kid my father wanted me to be a doctor. He was a wages clerk, so I had to be a doctor. I didn't want to be one, but that didn't make any difference. He beat me all the way through school until one day, when I was seventeen, I discovered I was stronger than he was. I slammed him on the jaw and left home.'

He fumbled for a cigarette with shaking hands and continued. 'There was a Chinese officer in charge of the prisoners at that coal mine they sent me to in Manchuria. Li, they called him. A little name for a little man. He had a complex about his size, so he didn't like me because I was big. I used to work in a low level, up to my knees in freezing water, for twelve hours a day. Sometimes if he didn't think I'd worked hard enough, he used to leave me in there all night when the others were brought up. I still get dreams about that. He used to turn up in the middle of the night and call down the shaft to me, his voice echoing along the passage. Other times he'd have me strung up and he'd beat me with a pick handle.'

Maria was crying softly, her head shaking from side to side. 'No more. Please, no more.'

Marlowe ignored her and went on. 'And what have I learned from all this? I'll tell you. It's quite simple really.' He raised a clenched fist. 'This! This is what counts. The boot and the fist. I've been shoved around by someone or other all my life. My father, Captain Li, O'Connor, or Monaghan. They're all the same breed, and they can only be handled in one way.'

She turned away blindly, and Magellan moved forward and put a hand on Marlowe's arm. There was a great pity in his face. 'I know what it's like to have a devil on your shoulder, but he's the one you've got to fight. Not the rest of the world.'

Marlowe nodded wearily. 'I think I'll have that bath now, Papa. I could do with it.'

He moved forward and paused, one foot on the bottom stair. 'Another thing, Papa. That job you were talking about. If it's still open I'll take it. O'Connor is beginning to annoy me. He reminds me of someone I once knew.'

The old man smiled, his whole face coming alive, and he nodded. 'That's fine, son. You go and have that bath and we'll talk about it afterwards.'

Marlowe turned and started to climb the stairs. His whole body was full of an inexpressible weariness. Already he was beginning to regret his decision, but he was committed to it. Whatever happened now he would not go back on his given word. He felt as if some strong force had him in its grip and was bearing him swiftly along to an unknown destination.

He shrugged and a half-smile came to his mouth. What the hell. He wasn't scared of O'Connor or Monaghan or any of them. His smile changed into a wide grin as he went into the bathroom. He felt almost sorry for O'Connor. He was certainly in for a hell of a surprise.

4

The morning was cold with no rain, and a trace of mist hung over the fields behind the house as Marlowe crossed the yard towards the old barn. He could hear voices inside, and he paused for a moment on the threshold to light a cigarette before going in.

Cold, clammy air enveloped him like a shroud, and he shivered. The place was brightly illuminated by several bulbs strung from an electric cable, and Maria Magellan and an old man were busy loading boxes and sacks on to a Bedford three-ton truck which stood in the centre of the barn. Two more were parked in the shadows down at the far end.

As he moved forward the girl turned quickly. 'Good morning,' she said.

'It's like an ice-box in here,' Marlowe told her.

She shrugged. 'The walls are three feet thick. Just what we need to store fruit.' She moved towards a table that stood against the wall and lifted a metal pot from a small electric stove. 'Coffee?'

He nodded briefly. 'Where's your father this morning?'

'In bed.' She made a tiny grimace. 'Rheumatism, and he isn't very pleased about it. He gets an attack now and then when the weather turns damp. I'll probably have to lock his door to keep him inside.'

He drank some of the scalding black coffee and grunted with pleasure as its warmth moved through him. He nodded towards the truck and the old man, still busy loading boxes. 'You keep early hours.'

'You have to in this game if you want to make a living,' she said.

'You should have awakened me and I'd have given you a hand,' he told her.

'Oh, don't worry,' she said. 'I shall do another morning. Just breaking you in gently.'

The old man approached, his gnarled hand busy with a pipe and tobacco pouch. He was wearing a greasy corduroy cap and an ancient patched suit. He looked seventy at least. 'That's the lot, Miss Maria,' he said in a cracked voice. 'I'll go over to the greenhouse now.'

Maria smiled warmly. 'All right, Dobie. Breakfast at nine.' He turned to go and she added quickly, 'Oh, Dobie, this is Hugh Marlowe. He's going to drive for us.'

The old man looked at Marlowe with vacant, watery eyes and nodded. Then he turned away, lighting his pipe as he went, and disappeared into the grey morning.

'Is he much use?' Marlowe asked. 'He looked pretty old to be still doing a day's work.'

Maria poured herself a cup of coffee and shrugged. 'If he stopped working he'd die. He's that kind of man. Anyway, he knows more about market gardening than any man I know. We wouldn't be without him.'

Marlowe helped himself to more coffee. 'He's still too old to be humping sacks of potatoes on to trucks. Another morning wake me.'

Her eyes flashed angrily. 'Don't worry, Mr Marlowe. I'll see you earn your money.'

He grinned and lit another cigarette. 'I'll earn it all right.'

He moved towards the truck and lifted the tailboard into place. 'What do I do with this lot?'

'One of two things,' she told him. 'Either sell the stuff at the market or go round the shops like Bill Johnson did yesterday.'

'Is there any point in going to the market?' he said. 'I thought O'Connor had everything sewed up there.'

She nodded. 'Just about, but there's one independent wholesaler left. Old Sam Granby. He's been ill for a long time and his nephew Tom has been in charge. Tom's mixed up with O'Connor, but the old man isn't. We heard yesterday that he might be back today. It's worth a try.'

Marlowe nodded. 'I'd better get cracking then.'

She frowned and took a slip of paper from her pocket. 'I nearly forgot this,' she said. Marlowe examined the paper. It was a list of various kinds of fruits and vegetables with prices marked beside them. 'You mustn't go below those prices,' she explained, 'otherwise we shan't make a profit.'

Marlowe grinned. 'That wouldn't do at all,' he said. 'Don't worry. I'll get the price you want.'

She took an old fur-lined jeep coat from a cupboard and threw it across to him. 'You'd better put it on,' she said. 'It can get pretty cold in the cab of that truck.'

He pulled on the coat and climbed up behind the wheel. As he slammed the door she moved a little nearer and added, 'Don't forget, Marlowe. Stay out of trouble.'

He pulled the starter and the engine roared into life. He grinned mockingly at her. 'Don't worry about me, angel. I hate trouble.'

Disbelief showed clearly on her face, and he released the handbrake and drove out into the yard before she could reply.

The journey into Barford took just under half an hour. For most of the way he drove with the side window down, the cool morning breeze fanning his cheek. He felt no particular anxiety about what might happen when he reached the market even though it was probable that Kennedy had already reported the happenings of the previous day to O'Connor.

The streets of Barford were quiet and deserted, but when he drove into the large cobbled square in the centre of the town he found thirty or forty trucks and vans parked. The place was a hive of activity and noise, with men passing rapidly between the vehicles pushing large handcarts loaded with produce.

Half-way along the south side of the square on the corner of a narrow street a large warehouse lifted into the sky. A yellow painted board stretched high across the face of the building carrying the legend: 'Inter-Allied Trading Corporation'. A few yards farther along on the same side of the square a faded wooden board indicated the premises of Sam Granby.

Marlowe parked the truck not far from O'Connor's place and threaded his way through the busy crowd of porters. There was a small loading ramp outside Sam Granby's warehouse, and as he walked towards it he saw Kennedy leaning against the large double door that led into the interior of the building, smoking a cigarette.

Kennedy's face was badly marked and his lips were bruised and swollen to several times their normal size. As Marlowe mounted the steps that led up on to the loading ramp Kennedy recognized him. For a moment he stared at Marlowe in astonishment and then an expression of fear came into his eyes. He turned and darted into the interior of the building. Marlowe paused long enough to light a cigarette and then followed him in.

Inside the warehouse several men worked busily packing apples into wooden boxes. There was a glass-fronted office at the top of a flight of old-fashioned iron stairs in one corner and Kennedy was clearly visible as he talked excitedly to someone who was sitting down.

Marlowe mounted the stairs and opened the door of the office. There were two other men present besides Kennedy. The one who sat behind the desk was young and dark haired with sharp, crafty eyes. The other reclined in an old easy chair, the springs of which sagged dangerously. He was the fattest man Marlowe had ever seen, with a great, fleshy face that carried an expression of perpetual good humour and candid blue eyes that sparkled merrily.

Kennedy turned quickly, an expression of alarm on his face and Marlowe smiled contemptuously. 'For Christ's sake, Kennedy, try not to look as though you're going to wet yourself each time you see me.'

An expression of rage appeared on Kennedy's face and he pushed past Marlowe, jerked open the door and disappeared down the stairs. The fat man chuckled explosively, his great frame shaking with mirth. 'Poor Kennedy,' he said in a peculiarly light voice. 'He can't take a joke. Never could.'

Marlowe ignored him and spoke to the man behind the desk. 'Where can I find Sam Granby?'

The young man sat back, a wary expression in his eyes. 'Across the square at the undertaker's,' he said. 'He died last night.' He showed his teeth in a mirthless grin. 'I'm his

45

nephew – Tom Granby. I'm the owner now.'

Marlowe nodded slowly. So much for Maria Magellan's hopes. 'I've got a load of stuff outside,' he said. 'Are you interested?'

Granby picked up a pencil and examined it thoughtfully. 'That depends. Who are you from?'

Marlowe tried to control his rising anger. 'You know damned well who I'm from, sonny,' he said. 'Let's stop fooling around.'

The fat man exploded into laughter again. 'That's good,' he wheezed. 'That's really very funny.'

Marlowe said coldly over his shoulder, 'Who asked you to stick your nose in?'

The face still smiled but there was a different expression in the eyes. Another chuckle shook the huge frame. 'That's even funnier. You'd better tell him, Tom.'

Granby cleared his throat and said, with obvious pleasure, 'This is my new partner – Mr O'Connor.'

Marlowe turned towards the fat man and looked him over contemptuously. 'So you're the great O'Connor?' he said at last.

O'Connor wiped his eyes with a large white handkerchief. 'And you're the bloke that knocked hell out of Kennedy yesterday.' His eyes flicked over Marlowe's massive frame and he nodded. 'I'd like to have seen that. You're a big man, son. A very big man.'

'But not so big that he can't be cut down to size,' Granby said viciously.

Marlowe turned, his left hand darting out. He grabbed Tom Granby by the shirt front and half dragged him across the desk. For a moment he looked coldly into the frightened eyes. 'The next time you cross me I'll stamp you into the ground, you worm,' he said. He released his grip and Granby fell back into his chair.

O'Connor shook his head and clicked his tongue. 'Very silly, Tom. You really asked for that.' He switched his glance back to Marlowe. 'Old man Magellan's washed up. A week from now he won't be able to pay your wages.'

Marlowe didn't even bother to reply. He turned and

walked towards the door. O'Connor moved surprisingly fast for a man of his bulk. He caught him by the arm and said, 'Let's be reasonable, son. I can always use a good man.'

Marlowe looked down at the podgy hand on his sleeve and said coldly, 'Take your paw off me.' O'Connor's hand dropped as if it had been stung and Marlowe looked straight into his face. 'I wouldn't cut you down if you were hanging, you fat pig.'

The tiny blue eyes filled with malevolence. For a moment they looked steadily at each other and then O'Connor smiled. 'All right, son,' he said. 'Have it your own way.'

As Marlowe opened the door he half turned. 'One more thing, O'Connor. Try to crowd me and you'll curse the day you were born. I promise you.' He closed the door quietly and descended the stairs.

Once outside he stood on the ramp for a moment, lighting a cigarette, and considered the problem. Obviously he would have to do the round of the retail shops that Bill Johnson had done the previous day. Somehow he didn't think O'Connor would leave that loophole open for long, if he hadn't already closed it.

He walked slowly back towards the truck. As he passed the loading bay at the front of O'Connor's warehouse he noticed Kennedy standing in a doorway talking to a young girl. She wore tight denim jeans and a hip-length leather driving jacket. Her face was round and soft like a young child's and framed in hair that was almost pure white, like soft flax glinting palely in the morning sun.

Kennedy said something to her and she looked up quickly towards Marlowe. He gazed steadily at her for several seconds and then continued across the front of the building towards the truck. He looked back once and she was still staring after him.

A little way along the narrow street that ran down one side of O'Connor's warehouse, Marlowe noticed a café sign and market men passing in and out. He was suddenly aware that he was hungry and he turned into the street and walked towards the café.

There was a narrow alley at the rear of O'Connor's warehouse and as he drew abreast of it he saw a crowd standing on the corner and heard voices raised in anger. He crossed the street quickly and shouldered his way through the crowd.

There was another loading bay at the rear of the building and four men stood arguing furiously on its edge. One of them was a Negro and on the ground at his feet stood a battered, fibre suitcase tied with string. The man who was doing most of the shouting was well over six feet tall with a chest like a barrel and a mane of black curly hair. He was swearing vilely with a pronounced Irish accent and he held up a clenched fist menacingly. 'We don't like spades round here,' he said. 'They make the place smell bad. Get back to bloody Jamaica where you came from.' He lifted his boot back and kicked the man's suitcase several feet through the air until it crashed against the far wall.

The Jamaican took a step forward and his fists clenched. For a moment Marlowe hoped he was going to strike the Irishman and then his chin dropped and he relaxed. He turned to step down from the ramp and one of the other men stuck out a foot and tripped him so that he fell heavily to the ground.

The big Irishman jumped down beside him, a huge grin on his face. 'That's where you belong, nigger. In the muck,' he said.

The Jamaican was on his feet like a cat. He moved forward in one beautiful fluid motion and slammed his fist hard against the Irishman's jaw. He went down as if he had been poleaxed.

He scrambled to his feet with a roar of rage and at the same moment his two friends jumped down from the loading bay and grabbed the Negro's arms from behind. 'Go on, Blacky,' one of them cried. 'Knock hell out of him.'

The Irishman stood back for a moment, wiping blood from his mouth, and then he moved forward, a smile of pleasure on his face. Marlowe turned and said to the crowd contemptuously, 'What kind of men are you? Isn't anyone going to give the bloke a hand?'

An old man in a battered corduroy cap and greasy raincoat turned to him. 'You must be new around here. It doesn't pay to interfere with Blacky Monaghan.'

There was a street cleaner's cart standing nearby with a brush and spade inside it. Marlowe picked up the spade and moved down the alley towards the four men.

As he approached, Monaghan turned towards him, surprise on his face. 'What the hell do you want?' he demanded truculently.

Marlowe ignored him. He hefted the spade in his right hand and spoke to the two men who were holding the Jamaican. They were looking at the spade, complete unbelief on their faces, and he said calmly, 'If you two don't get to hell out of here I'll break your arms.'

He swung the spade once through the air. The two thugs jumped back, horror on their faces. They released the Jamaican and scrambled up on to the loading bay.

The Negro smiled, showing even white teeth. 'Thanks a lot, friend,' he said in a soft, Jamaican voice. 'I'll remember that.'

Monaghan stood with his back against the wall, mouthing obscenities. 'I'll catch you without that spade, bucko, one of these dark nights,' he snarled. 'It'll be my turn then.'

Marlowe ignored him. He stood back against the loading bay, still gripping the spade, and smiled at the Negro. 'It's your turn now, pal.'

A grin of unholy joy crossed the Jamaican's face and he moved towards Monaghan. The Irishman spat and doubled his fists and a quiet voice said, 'Now then, what are you trying to do? Turn Barford into a frontier town?'

Marlowe turned his head quickly. The crowd at the end of the alley had melted away and a quiet, middle-aged man was approaching them. He wore a brown gaberdine raincoat and an old blue felt hat. A greying, tobacco-stained moustache added the finishing touch to a sad, spaniel face.

The Jamaican moved quickly to Marlowe's shoulder and whispered, 'Watch yourself. This one's a copper.'

Very carefully Marlowe slipped his right hand behind him and propped the spade up against the wall. He wasn't quite quick enough. The moustache twitched and a humorous expression appeared in the eyes. 'What are you going to do with that, son?' the policeman demanded. 'Plant your rose trees?'

Marlowe grinned amiably. 'How did you guess?'

The moustache twitched again and the policeman turned to Monaghan and said calmly, 'Get out of it you, before I run you in.'

Blackie glared and his mouth half opened as if he was about to speak and then he scrambled up on to the loading bay and disappeared into the warehouse.

The policeman turned to the Jamaican and said, 'Now then, Mac, what started it?'

The Jamaican shrugged. 'Oh, the usual thing, Mr Alpin. They just don't like having me around I guess.'

Alpin nodded soberly and turned his eye speculatively on Marlowe. 'What's your name, son? Where do you fit into this?'

Marlowe shrugged. 'There were three of them working him over. I just stepped in to see fair play. I drive a truck for Mr Magellan, of Litton. Marlowe's my name.'

Alpin nodded towards the spade. 'You certainly believe in shock tactics, don't you.' He shook his head. 'That's the way to end up in the dock on a capital charge.'

The Jamaican picked up his suitcase and they all walked towards the end of the alley. Alpin said, 'What are you going to do now, Mac?'

The Negro shook his head. 'I don't know, Mr Alpin. Maybe I'll try London again. It's hard enough for a white man to get a job in a rural area.'

Alpin nodded. 'Well, I hope you make out all right.' He produced a patent inhaler, inserted it in one nostril and sniffed deeply. 'That's better,' he observed. 'Damned hay fever again.' He blew his nose loudly into a khaki handkerchief and said, 'Well, I've got to be off. If I can do anything for you, Mac, don't hesitate to get in touch.' He nodded to Marlowe. 'Give my regards to Papa Magellan and tell him I was asking after him.' He started to move away and then he paused and added, 'And you keep out of Blacky Monaghan's way, especially on dark nights, and keep away from spades.' He turned without waiting for a reply and walked down towards the square, his raincoat flapping about his legs in the slight breeze.

The Jamaican said quietly, 'He's a good man. It's a pity there aren't more like him.' He sighed deeply and then turned with a smile and held out his hand. 'I haven't thanked you yet, friend. My name's Mackenzie – Henry Mackenzie. Most people just call me Mac.'

Marlowe grasped the proffered hand. 'Hugh Marlowe,' he said. He nodded towards the café. 'I was just going in for a coffee. How about joining me?'

Mac nodded and picked up his suitcase and they crossed the road and entered the café. The place was crowded, but they managed to find a small table by the window and Marlowe brought two coffees from the counter. He offered the Jamaican a cigarette. 'That was one hell of a smack on the jaw you gave Monaghan. You looked as if you knew how to use yourself.'

Mac grinned. 'I should do. I came over here as a professional boxer.'

'Do any good?' Marlowe asked.

The Jamaican shrugged. 'I was going great there for a year or two until the night I got in a clinch on the ropes with a guy and fell through. I fractured my foot.' He sighed. 'They managed to fix it, but when I started training again I found I was only good for one fast round before the pain started.'

'That's pretty rough luck,' Marlowe said.

The Jamaican grinned and sat back in his chair. 'Don't think I'm crying in my beer, man. Life's just a big wheel going round. Now I'm down, next time I go up.' He spread his hands. 'It's the law of nature.'

Marlowe grinned and nodded. 'Maybe you've got something there,' he said. 'What were you doing for O'Connor?'

Mac shrugged. 'Anything that came to hand, packing fruit, making up loads. He took me on as a truck driver.'

'What did you think of him?' Marlowe said.

The smile faded from the Jamaican's face. 'I didn't like him. They're a bad lot over there. If it hadn't been for Miss Jenny I'd have left long ago. She was the only one that treated me decent.'

'And who's Miss Jenny?' Marlowe asked him.

'O'Connor's niece,' Mac said. 'She's like a flower on a dung heap over there.' He laughed shortly and added, 'One good thing. There isn't a man in that crowd who'd dare to lay a finger on her. O'Connor would sure have his scalp.' He glanced across at a clock on the wall. 'I guess I'd better be moving. There's a train for London in twenty minutes.'

Marlowe reached across and pulled him back down into his seat. 'Why go to London?' he said. 'I can get you a job right here.'

Mac frowned. 'You mean that, friend? What kind of a job?'

Marlowe pushed his cigarettes across. 'Truck driving, but I warn you. It might get a little rough. I work for a man called Magellan, in Litton. O'Connor is trying to put him out of business.'

'O'Connor put quite a few people out of business. How are you going to stop him doing the same thing to you?'

Marlowe held up a clenched fist. 'There are ways,' he said. 'There are ways.'

A slow smile appeared on the Jamaican's face. He held out his hand. 'Mr Marlowe, it'll be a pleasure working with you.'

'Right,' Marlowe said in satisfaction. 'Let's get out of here.'

They left the café and went down the street and back into the square. Men were still working busily on every side and when they reached the truck Marlowe said, 'Climb in. You do the driving. We'll go back to Litton and I'll introduce you to Papa Magellan.'

Suddenly he was aware of a hand on his arm. He turned and looked down into the blue eyes of the girl with the flaxen hair. They looked at each other without speaking for a brief moment and he was conscious of a sudden dryness in

52

his throat and a crawling sensation in the pit of his stomach. 'Mr Marlowe?' she said.

He nodded and cleared his throat. 'That's me. What can I do for you?'

'I'm Jenny O'Connor,' she said, 'Mr O'Connor's niece.'

Mac leaned out of the cab and said, 'Hallo, Miss Jenny.'

She glanced up and there was pain on her face. 'I heard what happened. I'm really sorry, Mac. What are you going to do?'

He smiled. 'I'll make out, Miss Jenny. I'm going to work for Mr Magellan, at Litton.'

Her eyes clouded over and she turned to Marlowe and there was urgency in her voice. 'But that makes it even worse. Please, Mr Marlowe, you must go away. Believe me, I know my uncle. He can't bear to be crossed. He'll stop at nothing to put Mr Magellan out of business. Any outsider who gets involved will only end up by getting hurt.'

Marlowe shook his head. 'No man can play God for ever and expect to get away with it, Miss O'Connor.'

'But he'll break you,' she said desperately. 'I've seen him do it to other people.'

'I don't break easily,' Marlowe told her. For a moment it seemed as if she would speak again and then her shoulders drooped and she turned away. 'Thanks for the warning, anyway,' Marlowe said.

He stood watching her as she walked back to the warehouse and went inside. He climbed up into the cab beside Mac and said, 'Well, now we know where we stand. Let's go, boy.'

As they moved away Marlowe turned his head and looked back towards the warehouse in time to see Kennedy, Monaghan and O'Connor emerge from the interior and stand on the ramp gazing after them. For a brief moment he had them in view and then Mac turned the truck into the main road and they roared out of the town, back towards Litton.

5

Marlowe was sitting on the end of Papa Magellan's bed. It was just after nine o'clock and the old man was finishing a hearty breakfast that Maria had brought to him on a tray. A light drift of rain pattered against the window and Magellan cursed and said, 'More rain, more rheumatism. It's a vicious circle and the whole damned winter still to come.'

Marlowe grinned sympathetically. 'Never mind, Papa,' he said. 'A couple of days in bed will do you a power of good.'

Magellan snorted. 'Nothing doing. That's what Maria thinks I need, but there's work to do and I'm the only one who can do it. This afternoon I've got to go round the market gardeners picking up produce and seeing how the land lies. Who knows what O'Connor is getting up to while I'm lying here in idleness.'

The door opened and Maria came in with a coffee pot and some cups on a tray. She filled two cups, gave one to her father and the other to Marlowe. 'How's Mac managing?' he asked her.

'Oh, fine,' she said. 'He helped me to put a spare bed in your room and I've left him unpacking.'

'What do you think of him?' Marlowe said.

'He's a good boy,' Papa Magellan cut in. 'I can always tell. He's got a good heart, that one.'

Maria nodded. 'I agree with papa. He's a fine man. I trust him. I felt it the moment I looked at him. He's not the kind who would ever let you down.'

For a moment a feeling that was suspiciously like jealousy moved in Marlowe. He gave her a twisted grin and said, 'Not like me at all.'

An expression of pain appeared on her face. 'Please, I didn't mean it to sound like that.'

He held up a hand. 'It doesn't matter. It doesn't matter at all.' When he turned to Papa Magellan he saw to his surprise, that the old man had a sly smile on his face. 'I'll take that load round the shops now, Papa,' Marlowe told him. 'Put Mac on the coal delivery run. As soon as I get back, I'll give him a hand.'

'Maybe I should get up and go round with the boy myself,' Papa Magellan said. 'He may find it a little strange at first.'

'You'll do nothing of the kind,' Maria said firmly. 'You can stay in bed and do as you're told for a change.'

'But Maria, there's work to be done,' the old man protested.

Marlowe shook his head and grinned. 'I'll leave you two to argue it out.' He grinned at the old man. 'Might as well give in, Papa. She can be pretty determined when she wants to be.' He closed the door quickly as the argument flared up again and went along to his bedroom.

Mac was unpacking his case and he looked up and smiled as Marlowe entered the room. 'Man, it was my lucky day today.'

Marlowe grinned. 'I thought you'd fit in here all right.' He lit a cigarette and went on, 'I'm going out with that load of stuff again. I'll try the retail shops and see what I can get rid of, but I don't feel too happy about it. O'Connor must know what's going on by now.'

Mac frowned and shook his head. 'He didn't exactly take me into his confidence. I hadn't even heard of Mr Magellan until I met you this morning.'

Marlowe nodded slowly. 'You're going to do the coal delivery run for the rest of the day. It shouldn't be too difficult. I'll be back by lunchtime and you can let me know how you're making out.'

Mac smiled and half saluted. 'Okay, boss,' he said. Marlowe grinned and left him to finish his unpacking.

As he drove back towards Barford it disturbed him to realize that in some inexorable way he seemed to be taking control of everything. He was beginning to get involved and he hadn't intended that to happen at all. For a little while he considered the point and then he pushed it firmly out of his mind and concentrated on the job in hand.

Maria had given him a list of the shops Bill Johnson had

done business with on the previous day. The first one was on a new housing estate on the very edge of Barford and Marlowe made straight for it.

The shop was a greengrocer's, a fine, red-brick, double-fronted building on the end of a large parade. When he went inside the place was deserted. He stood at the counter as the jangling of the door bell faded away and waited. After a moment or two, a man emerged from a rear door wiping his mouth with a napkin. He smiled cheerfully. 'Sorry to keep you. We have a late breakfast, you know. We're just finishing.'

Marlowe nodded. 'That's all right,' he said. 'I'm from Magellan's, of Litton. Our other man was round here yesterday. I thought you might be interested in some more stuff today.'

The grocer looked puzzled. 'I don't understand,' he said, 'your man's been round already this morning.'

Marlowe answered him automatically. 'I must have got the lists mixed up. He's working one part of the town and I'm supposed to be covering the other. We've probably got you down twice.'

The grocer smiled and said amiably, 'Never mind, young man. At the prices you're quoting this morning you won't have any difficulty in selling everything you've got.'

Marlowe forced a smile to his lips. 'I hope so. We need big sales to make it profitable.' He moved towards the door. 'Anyway, thanks a lot. I'll sort the mistake out with my friend when I see him.'

He got back into the cab of the truck and sat with his hands resting lightly on the wheel and stared out through the windscreen. He was seething with rage. When he looked down he saw that his hands were trembling and he gripped the wheel and swore violently. As the black, killing rage swept through him he hung on to the wheel and closed his eyes.

After a few minutes he felt a little better. He lit a cigarette and leaned back in the seat to consider the position. So Bill Johnson had played Judas? O'Connor must have discovered what was going on during the previous day.

That was the real reason why Blacky Monaghan and his thugs had waylaid Johnson at the roadside café. They must have slapped him around a little until he had agreed to play things their way.

Marlowe leaned forward and pulled the starter. As the engine coughed into life he reflected that it wouldn't have taken a great deal of persuasion to make a rat like Johnson agree to do as he was told. All men had their price. That was the first great lesson and it was the knowing of it that made men like O'Connor so successful. The one thing that rankled above everything else was the fact that all this had been planned. O'Connor must have been laughing up his sleeve during their meeting in Tom Granby's office.

After making another half-dozen calls he turned the truck back towards Litton. Everywhere he went it was the same story. Johnson had already called and his prices were heavily reduced. For the moment O'Connor had beaten them.

As he passed the roadside café on the outskirts of Barford he glanced idly across to the car park and saw Bill Johnson come out and walk towards a truck painted in a familiar yellow. Marlowe pulled into the side of the road and jumped down to the ground.

Johnson was reaching up to open the door of his cab when Marlowe grabbed him by the shoulder and spun him round. Abject fear showed on his face and he opened his mouth to scream. Marlowe hit him with all his force in the pit of the stomach. 'You rat,' he said bitterly. 'You dirty little rat.'

Johnson doubled over and sank to the ground. Marlowe lifted his foot back to deliver a final blow when there was a shout from behind him. He swung round and saw Monaghan and his two friends emerging from the café.

For a moment he wanted to stay and then discretion moved him to turn and run back across the road to his truck. As the engine drowned the cries of rage in the background, he reflected grimly that there would be other times. As he moved into top gear a grin of satisfaction appeared on his face. One thing was certain. Bill Johnson wouldn't forget him in a hurry.

As he pulled up outside the farmhouse door Papa Magellan appeared and stood on the top step waiting for him. Marlowe jumped down from the cab and as he approached, shook his head. 'No good, Papa,' he said. 'O'Connor hasn't wasted any time.'

The old man nodded and said heavily, 'You'd better come inside and tell me all about it.'

As they went into the living-room Maria appeared from the kitchen, wiping her hands on an apron. There was hope on her face and it died rapidly as she looked at her father. 'What is it, Papa?' she asked. 'What happened?'

The old man waved her to silence. 'Go on, son,' he told Marlowe.

Marlowe told them everything that had occurred. When he had finished Maria exploded with rage. 'Wait till I see Bill Johnson again,' she cried. 'I'll give him something to remember me by.'

Papa Magellan looked puzzled and there was pain on his face. 'Bill Johnson was a good boy,' he said. 'I don't understand. What can have happened to him?'

Marlowe shook his head impatiently. He held up his hand and rubbed his thumb across his index finger. 'Money, Papa. The only thing that really counts. With it, you're somebody. Without it, you're just nothing.'

'No!' Maria cried. 'I won't accept that. It isn't true.'

'For God's sake grow up,' Marlowe told her. 'Money means power. With it you can do anything. Money and fear. They have the greatest effect on men. Bill Johnson was weak and he was afraid. They threatened him and they offered him money. Of course he accepted.'

The old man sighed deeply and there was an air of hopelessness about him. 'What do we do now?' he asked. 'If we can't find a market we're finished.'

'You won't find one round here,' Marlowe told him forcibly. 'O'Connor only has to undercut your prices and he can afford to do that until you're broke.'

The old man managed a wry smile. 'And that won't take long, boy.'

There was a silence for a space before Maria said slowly,

'What about Birmingham? Why can't we take the stuff there?'

Marlowe shook his head, 'O'Connor has too many contacts. He could follow every move we made, undercut us at every turn.'

The old man nodded emphatically. 'Hugh is right, Maria. Birmingham is no good.'

Marlowe frowned as an idea suddenly came to him. 'What about London?' he said. 'Covent Garden. O'Connor is strictly a provincial. He can't throw much weight around there.'

Papa Magellan shook his head, 'It's too far.' Marlowe started to protest and the old man held up a hand. 'No, listen to me, son. Most of our produce is perishable. We're dealing in soft fruit a lot at the moment. It's got to be delivered first thing in the morning, so they can get it out to the shops fresh and in good condition.'

'Where's the problem?' Marlowe demanded. 'We drive to London through the night. It fits in beautifully. O'Connor won't even know what we're up to.'

Maria looked dubious. 'I don't know, Hugh, it's a long drive. Probably two hundred miles. You'd be taking on quite a job.'

Marlowe shrugged. 'What's two hundred miles. The roads will be empty. It'll be as easy as falling off a log.'

He looked from Maria to her father. The old man still looked uncertain and Marlowe said impatiently, 'For God's sake, Papa, this is your only chance. At least give it a try.'

The old man slapped a hand against his knee and stood up. 'By God, you're right,' he cried, eyes flashing. 'At least we'll go down fighting.' He took his jacket down from behind the door and pulled it on. 'We'll give that pig a run for his money yet.'

'Now where do you think you're going, Papa?' Maria demanded.

He held up his hand and his voice was stern. 'Maria, don't try to interfere. I'm going out in the other truck. I've got to make the rounds of the market gardeners to let them know we have things under control. Another thing, we need more

59

produce. If Hugh is going to drive all the way to London we must make it worth while.'

'But your meal is nearly ready, Papa,' she told him. 'You can't go now.'

'So I have the meal when I come back,' he replied. 'Is that such a hardship when our livelihood is at stake?'

He walked out of the room and the front door closed with a bang. Marlowe laughed. 'The old boy's still got plenty of starch left in him,' he observed.

Maria nodded. 'Papa can be pretty determined when he gets set on a thing. He's twice the man O'Connor will ever be.'

There was an awkward silence for a few moments and Maria played nervously with her apron. Rain had started to fall again and tapped on the window with ghostly fingers. She laughed self-consciously. 'It's rather a sad sound, isn't it?'

Marlowe remembered the many times he had lain on the cot in his cell listening to that same sound and longing to be free. 'It's just about the saddest sound in the world,' he said, with feeling.

For a brief moment they were very close. It was as if each had discovered in the other something they had not realized existed. A warm smile blossomed on Maria's face and she said, 'Come into the kitchen and I'll make you a cup of tea. You've had a hard morning.'

He followed her along the corridor and into the large, old-fashioned farm kitchen, warm with the smell of cooking. He sat on the edge of the table, swinging a leg and smoking a cigarette and felt at peace in a way that he hadn't experienced for a long time.

He watched her as she moved about the room, preparing the tea. Her limbs were softly rounded and as she bent down to pick up a cloth, her dress tightened showing the sweeping curve of her thigh and accentuating her large hips. Real childbearing hips, he mused to himself.

His thoughts drifted idly to Jenny O'Connor with her boyish slimness and he tried to compare the two women. He decided it was impossible. Jenny had a tremendous surface attractiveness, something completely animal that gripped a man by the bowels like a fever, lighting a fire that could only be extinguished by full and complete possession.

With Maria he knew it would be something very different. A sensuality that smouldered deep inside, ready to burst into a flame which could never be extinguished. She was a woman who would demand much, but who would give greatly in return.

She turned from the stove and handed him his tea. Her smile was like a lamp switching on inside her, illuminating her whole face. 'I think I owe you an apology, Hugh,' she said.

It was the second time within half an hour that she had used his Christian name. He frowned slightly. 'What are you talking about?'

She coloured and nervously played with her hands. 'I've been pretty unpleasant. You see, somehow I got the impression that you weren't really interested in our problems. I thought you were just using us because you needed a job.'

'And what makes you think I'm not?' he demanded.

That wonderful deep smile turned on again. 'Now, I know you're doing everything you can to help Papa. You've proved it.'

Marlowe sipped his tea and schooled his face to steadiness. Why did she have to put her own interpretation on everything he did? Couldn't she see that everything he had done so far had been done because he didn't like being pushed around? He was bitterly angry and he stood up and walked quickly to the window. He had to clench his teeth to keep himself from making an angry reply and yet, in his heart, he knew that it wasn't Maria he was annoyed with. It was himself. In some queer way he was sorry that he was not the kind of man that she believed him to be.

She moved beside him and placed a hand on his arm. 'What is it, Hugh?' she said. 'What's the matter?'

Her faint, womanly odour filled his nostrils and he was acutely aware of her physically. He turned abruptly, his hands reaching out and grasping her arms, and an answering flame flared in her eyes. At that moment the front door opened and Mac shouted, 'Hugh, are you in, boy? We got trouble.'

Marlowe released her and turned to the door as the Jamaican entered. There was excitement on his face and he pushed his cap back and brushed sweat from his brow. 'Man, am I glad you're here.'

'What's happened?' Marlowe demanded. 'Don't tell me O'Connor's started up in the coal business?'

Mac nodded. 'That's it, boy. That guy Kennedy who used to work here. He's delivering coal in the village. I've made several calls on farms and they've all told me the same story. Kennedy called today and told them Papa Magellan had given up the coal delivery side and that he'd taken over.'

'But he can't do that,' Maria cried. Her eyes filled with tears and she sank down into a chair. 'It isn't fair, Hugh. It isn't fair. This will be the finish of Papa.'

Marlowe gave her shoulder a hurried squeeze. 'Don't worry, angel,' he told her. 'I'll fix that rat Kennedy once and for all. He won't show his face round here again in a hurry when I get through with him.'

She raised her head at once, an expression of fear on her face. 'No, Hugh, please. No trouble. I'm scared what might happen.' He smiled once reassuringly and hurried out of the house, Mac at his heels.

It was raining quite heavily as they drove down into the village. They cruised through several streets without any luck and after ten minutes Marlowe was cursing steadily. 'Where the hell is he?' he demanded.

Mac shrugged. 'We can't be sure, Hugh. He may be calling on some of the outlying farms.'

At that moment a yellow truck turned out of a side street and passed them going in the opposite direction. Marlowe turned into a side street and reversed quickly. As they drove back along the main street he said to Mac, 'Did he spot us?'

Mac shook his head. 'Didn't even notice us. Too busy watching where he was going.'

The yellow truck slowed down and turned into a side street and Marlowe followed. A few yards past a public house there was a piece of waste land and Kennedy drove on to it and parked the truck. As they drove past, he climbed down and walked back to the public house.

'Gone for his lunchtime pint,' Marlowe said.

Mac nodded. 'What are you going to do?'

Marlowe had been examining the yellow truck closely with a slight frown. A smile appeared on his face and he started to laugh. 'I've just had a flash of genius,' he said. 'You wait here for me.'

He jumped down from the cab and walked back to the yellow truck. He paused for a moment and looked carefully about him to make sure that he wasn't observed. He jerked open the door of the cab, reached inside and pulled on a certain lever, and closed the door again. He turned and hurried back to Mac.

As he approached the truck, the Jamaican was leaning out, a delighted expression on his face. 'Man oh man, but that should fix him good.'

Marlowe turned and looked back. O'Connor's first venture into the coal business had obviously been hastily planned because the truck Kennedy was using was an hydraulic tipper. As Marlowe watched, the back slowly lifted into the air and sacks of coal started to topple. Inexorably, the back continued to rise until the last bag of coal had fallen to the road. At the very moment that happened, there was a cry of dismay from the public house and Kennedy emerged from the doorway.

Marlowe climbed up behind the wheel and started the engine. He reversed the truck and drove back towards the scene of the disaster. As they approached he slowed down and leaned out of the window. 'Having trouble, Kennedy?' he inquired.

Kennedy turned and his expression of dismay changed to one of fury. 'You bastard,' he shouted. 'O'Connor will fix you for this.'

Marlowe ignored the threat. 'Just give him a message from me,' he said. 'Tell him he'd better not try this stunt again. I shan't play games next time.' He moved into gear and drove away before Kennedy could reply.

When the truck rolled to a halt inside the barn, Maria came running from the house, tremendous anxiety on her face. 'What happened?' she demanded. 'You didn't start any trouble, Hugh? Please say you didn't.'

Marlowe grinned. 'Everything went fine,' he said. 'I never even laid a finger on Kennedy. He had an accident as a matter of fact. All his coal got spilled on to the road. He was in a bit of a mess when we left.'

Relief showed on her face and something suspiciously like laughter sparkled in her eyes. 'You don't think he'll be back again?'

Marlowe shook his head gravely. 'No, somehow I don't think he will.'

She nodded. 'Thank goodness. Papa's back. I haven't told him anything yet. I didn't want to worry him.' She smiled brightly. 'Anyway, there's a meal ready. Hurry and get washed before it's spoiled.'

During the meal Mac told Papa Magellan and Maria in detail what had happened to Kennedy. He was a natural story-teller and had them both laughing heartily before he had finished. Afterwards, over coffee, they discussed the projected London trip. Mac was in full agreement with the idea. 'Seems to me it's the one way to putting one over on O'Connor,' he observed.

'I'm glad you agree,' Marlowe told him, 'because you're the one who'll have to make the trip.'

There was a momentary surprise in Mac's eyes that was immediately replaced by something like understanding. Maria said in puzzlement, 'But why shouldn't you go as well, Hugh? Wouldn't it be easier with two drivers?'

Papa Magellan cut in hastily. 'Hugh has his reasons, Maria. If he doesn't want to go to London that's his affair. Let it rest.'

Maria sat back in her chair, frowning and Marlowe said easily, 'What about the market gardeners, Papa? What have they got to say?'

The old man shrugged and looked grave. 'I was right about O'Connor. He's been round to most of the people I deal with, offering to buy direct and at much better prices.'

'How many have accepted?' Marlowe asked.

Magellan shrugged. 'Not as many as you would think. They're pretty shrewd, these men. Most of them are intelligent enough to realize that he won't pay them such fancy prices when he's squeezed me out of business. The majority have stuck with me, but I've had to guarantee them a price.'

'That means you've got to pay them whatever happens?' Maria said.

The old man nodded and Marlowe frowned. 'In other words, the only person who's risking anything is you?'

Papa Magellan smiled. 'I have enough ready cash to guarantee the first couple of loads. But if anything goes wrong . . .' he shrugged and left the sentence unfinished.

Mac sighed and got to his feet. 'I guess that means we can't afford any mistakes,' he observed.

At that moment there was the sound of a vehicle. As the engine was cut, Marlowe moved to the window and looked out. A green Jaguar was standing outside. The door opened and a slim, boyish figure slid gracefully out of the upholstered seat. 'Now I wonder what *she* wants?' Maria said softly at his shoulder.

It was Jenny O'Connor.

6

As the front door bell rang they looked at each other. After a moment or two, Marlowe said, 'It might be a good idea if someone let the girl in.'

'Maria!' Papa Magellan said in a tone that admitted no denial. 'Answer the door.'

Maria went without further argument. They heard the murmur of voices in the hall and then Jenny O'Connor stood hesitating in the doorway. Maria looked over her shoulder, a hostile expression on her face. 'She wants to speak to Hugh,' she said.

Jenny O'Connor smiled and shook her head quickly. 'No, please don't anyone leave. What I have to say concerns you all.'

She was wearing a tailored skirt and a brown suede jacket and her slim legs were encased in the sheerest of nylon stockings. Marlowe was conscious of the same crawling sensation in his stomach and the dryness in throat he had experienced during their first meeting. He swallowed hard and said: 'What did you want to see me about, Miss O'Connor?'

She coloured with embarrassment and dropped her eyes. For a moment she seemed at a loss for words and Papa Magellan with old-fashioned Latin courtliness took her by the arm and led her to a chair. 'Sit down, my dear,' he said. 'You have no enemies here.'

Maria snorted with anger and folded her arms. Her lips were pressed tightly together as if to bottle up her rage. Jenny O'Connor smiled at her. 'Please, Miss Magellan. Don't condemn me until you've heard what I have to say.'

There was silence as they waited for her to carry on. She seemed to experience even greater difficulty in speaking, but quite suddenly, the words poured from her like a torrent. 'I know Mr O'Connor is my uncle and my action in coming here must seem very strange, but I can't stand by and see all this trouble and violence going on without a stop.'

Maria made an impatient sound and Marlowe said gently, 'What do you suggest we do about it, Miss O'Connor?'

She looked up slowly and there was great trouble in her candid blue eyes. 'Mr Magellan must sell,' she said simply.

There was a brief moment of astonished silence and then Maria threw back her head and laughed. 'So this is why you have come to see us,' she said. 'What do you think we are, fools?'

Papa Magellan turned on her angrily. 'Maria, if you cannot keep quiet you must leave the room.' For a second her eyes challenged him and then she turned and rushed out into the corridor, slamming the door behind her. Magellan turned to Jenny and inclined his head. 'I am sorry, Miss O'Connor. You must forgive my daughter. She has worried a great deal about this matter.'

'Why should Mr Magellan sell out now?' Marlowe asked her, his eyes fixed on her face.

'Because if he doesn't my uncle will break him,' she replied. 'Kennedy returned an hour ago. When my uncle heard what you had done he was furious. Insane with rage. I've never seen him so angry.'

'Did he send you here?' Marlowe asked her.

She smiled sadly and shook her head. 'Mr Marlowe, my uncle has very firm ideas about a woman's place. He never allows me to meddle in his business affairs. I love driving and he's humoured me to the extent of allowing me to take out one of the trucks now and then.'

Papa Magellan frowned slightly. 'May I inquire then, what has brought you here this morning?'

She stood up and walked over to the window and stood staring out at the rain. 'I hate to see useless violence,' she said quietly. 'There's been too much already. If this state of affairs goes on there will be more.' She turned quickly and said, 'I know my uncle is in the wrong in this matter, but he has money and power and a large organization. He can put you out of business by using methods which are quite legal.'

Marlowe smiled softly. 'And what if we don't intend to be put out of business?'

'But what else can you do?' There was real concern on her face. 'He has stopped you from dealing with the market. This morning he's blocked off your retail shops outlet by undercutting your prices. All quite legal.' She appeared to hesitate and then went on, 'I must sound like a complete traitor telling you this, but I know that he's started to approach the market gardeners you deal with, Mr Magellan. He can offer better prices than you can. How can you possibly stand up to pressure like this?'

Mac grinned and said impulsively, 'There are more ways of killing a cat than drowning, Miss Jenny. Maybe we've got a trick or two left that might surprise your uncle.'

Marlowe kicked him sharply on the ankle as Jenny O'Connor's face clouded with puzzlement. 'It was good of you to come here,' he said. 'But I'm afraid there's no prospect of us selling out. Your uncle started this affair. He'll have to stick it out to the bitter end now.'

Her shoulders drooped again as they had done when they had last met. She looked completely defeated. 'I seem to have wasted my time.' She raised her head and forced a smile. 'I'm glad to have met you, Mr Magellan. Believe me, if I have any influence on my uncle at all, I'll use it to try and bring this sorry business to an end.'

She nodded to Mac and moved out into the hall. Marlowe went with her. As he opened the door of the Jaguar and handed her in she said, 'I seem to have made rather a fool of myself.'

He shook his head and replied gently, 'You could never do that.'

She looked surprised and paused for a moment, her hands resting on the wheel. 'You seem to know a lot about me?'

He nodded and said calmly, 'I'd know a lot more if you'd let me see you tonight. Perhaps we could have a drink and a bite to eat somewhere?'

She stared steadily at him and a slow, grave smile appeared on her face. 'You're a strange man,' she said.

He grinned. 'I get even stranger the longer you know me. Shall I see you tonight?'

She hastily scribbled in a tiny leather diary and tore out the page. 'There's my address,' she said, handing it to him. 'Pick me up at about seven-thirty.' She pressed the starter button and as the superb engine began to tick over, said, 'You'd better go in now. You're getting rather wet.'

He stood with the slip of paper between his fingers and watched the car disappear into the distance and then he turned and went back into the house.

'And what was all that about?' Maria demanded, eyes flashing, when he returned to the living-room.

He grinned and held up the slip of paper. 'The lady's address,' he said. 'I'm taking her out tonight.'

For a moment only there was an expression of complete dismay on her face, but it was quickly replaced by one of fury. 'What exactly do you think you're playing at?' she demanded.

He ignored her and went over to the sideboard and helped himself to brandy. He turned and silently toasted the three of them and tossed it down his throat in one quick gulp. As the warmth moved through him he grinned in satisfaction. 'Yes, I'm going to take the lady out tonight,' he said. 'We'll spend the evening in Barford where I'll be nice and conspicuous.'

Understanding came to Papa Magellan and Mac at the same time. 'You're going to act as a decoy,' the Jamaican said.

As Marlowe nodded, the old man shook his head vigorously. 'It's insane. Barford at night-time will be pretty unhealthy. Monaghan and his thugs must be waiting for a chance to get you in a dark alley.'

Marlowe grinned. 'That's the idea. The whole mob will be concentrating on me, wondering what the hell I'm doing in Barford in the first place. They'll probably spend so much time trying to find an answer, they won't get around to any rough stuff.'

'And is that the only reason you're going?' Maria asked, her eyes fixed on him.

'What other reason could there be?' he told her. For a moment their eyes were locked together and then he turned and said, 'Come on, Mac. We've got to get that truck checked and loaded for your big trip.' Together they left the room and Marlowe was conscious of the girl's eyes burning into him as he went.

She was perfectly right, of course. There was another reason for seeing Jenny O'Connor, and with her woman's intuition Maria had guessed it. As Marlowe alighted from the bus in the main square at Barford that evening he saw himself reflected in a mirror and he shook his head and decided that he would never understand women.

Maria had carefully brushed and pressed the tweed suit he had been given on his release from Wandsworth and his shirt was gleaming white and freshly ironed. The suit didn't look too bad at all, he decided. At least it had been made to measure and fitted in all the right places.

As he walked along the pavement a church clock struck the hour and he checked his watch. It was seven o'clock and Mac was starting for London at eight. It would be dark enough then, Marlowe decided, looking up at the sky.

He had no difficulty in finding her address. It was a gay mews flat in a small courtyard not far from the square. The window boxes were painted bright red and one or two flowers still bloomed in them. He pressed the bell push and glanced about him as he waited. There was no sign of her car and he listened to the silence from within with a slight frown, wondering whether he had made a mistake.

As he reached in his pocket for the slip of paper he heard a footfall and the door opened. She stood there smiling at him. She was wearing a long red housecoat of heavy silk and her hair gleamed like spun gold. She stood to one side. 'Come in, Mr Marlowe. You're a little early.'

She led the way across an oak-panelled hall and into a beautiful room. Rose carpeting completely covered the floor and cleverly concealed lights tinted the walls the same colour. A large fire flickered in a superb Adam fireplace and rich velvet curtains were drawn across the windows, somehow cutting the room off from the outside world. She motioned him into a large, wing-backed chair and went across to a cocktail cabinet and poured two drinks from a shaker. 'I had these ready mixed,' she said, as she handed him one of the glasses. 'Martinis. I hope you like them.'

Marlowe nodded. 'An old favourite of mine.' He sipped his drink and leaned back in the chair and watched her.

She curled up on a long, high-backed settee that matched his chair, and smiled. 'There isn't any great rush,' she said. 'I've booked dinner at a place I know a few miles out of Barford. Unfortunately, something's gone wrong with the car. The garage have taken it away. It's nothing serious. They promised to have it fixed in an hour.'

He nodded and offered her a cigarette. 'That's too bad.' As he sat back in his chair he smiled and added: 'However, I'm not complaining. This will do very nicely. It's a beautiful room.'

She nodded and got up to replenish his drink. 'I like beautiful things,' she said. 'They make me feel good. Life can be so drab.'

'The trouble is they all cost money,' he said as she came back with his drink.

She smiled. 'Oh, I don't know. Some things are still pretty inexpensive.' She flicked a switch by the fireplace and plunged the room into half darkness. 'Firelight for instance.' She settled back on the settee. 'It's one of the few things that haven't changed.'

Marlowe was puzzled. 'Changed?' he said.

'From the old days.' She pillowed her head on one arm like a little girl and turned towards the fire and her eyes glinted, amber and gold. 'When I was a little girl I can remember having tea with my father in his study at four o'clock on Autumn afternoons. It was a special treat, something to look forward to. It was a wonderful room, lined with books and there was always an immense fire. The maid used to bring in tea and hot muffins on a tray and my father would let me be hostess.' She chuckled. 'I loved handling the silver teapot and the beautiful china cups. There was a special intimacy about it with the dead leaves falling outside the long window and the shadows moving from the corners of the room.' She shivered and there was an utter desolation in her voice. Marlowe didn't speak and for a moment there was silence and then she said briskly, 'But that was a long time ago. Before the flood.'

Marlowe frowned. There was something he didn't understand here. 'What happened?' he said.

She shrugged. 'My father lost his money. He got mixed up in some financial swindle.' She hesitated and said briefly, 'He blew his brains out.'

'I'm sorry,' Marlowe told her. 'That was a rough break.'

She smiled and shrugged. 'The only trouble about being born into money is that you find it impossible to do without it. It means one has to look for a solution and sometimes it may be rather unpleasant.'

The picture was becoming a little clearer. 'And you found your solution?'

She smiled wistfully. 'Solutions are usually hard to come by. How old do you think I am, Mr Marlowe?'

He shrugged. 'It's hard to say. Eighteen – nineteen.'

She laughed. 'I'm twenty-eight next month. When I was seventeen I married a wealthy man because I wanted security. He gave me ten years of hell. He was unfaithful, a drunkard and when the mood was on him, he wasn't above knocking me around. I put up with him because I didn't have the courage to go out and face life on my own. When he died in a car crash last year I thought I was free. Unfortunately he left nothing but debts.'

'And that's when O'Connor stepped in?' Marlowe said.

She nodded. 'That's right. He was my father's half-brother. I knew very little about him. I believe there was some scandal when he was young and he had to leave home. He got in touch with me six months ago and offered to provide for me.'

'And you accepted,' Marlowe said.

She shrugged. 'Why not? I'm weak.' She indicated the room with a gesture of one hand. 'He's good to me. In some queer way of his own he's proud of me. He likes people to know that I'm his niece. I suppose he's looking for a veneer of respectability now that he's rich.'

'Are you happy?' Marlowe asked her.

She smiled sadly. 'Isn't it the Bible which tells us we must pay for our weaknesses, Mr Marlowe?' She laughed in a strange way and reached for a cigarette from a silver box on a small table beside her. 'I have everything I want. Everything. It's just that I get so lonely at times. So damned lonely.'

For a long moment they stared at each other and the terrible dryness clutched at Marlowe's throat again. As the firelight flared up, illuminating her face, he saw tears glisten in her eyes and then the cigarette fell from her fingers and her face crumpled up like a child's. 'So lonely,' she repeated. 'So damned lonely.'

Marlowe got to his feet, a terrible vital force rushing through him. There was a great roaring in his ears and as he stumbled forward, her arms reached out and pulled him down. Her mouth fastened hungrily on his and she moaned his name once. As his hands moved over her she gave a cry of ecstasy and her fingers clawed at him like a tigress as the fury swelled to envelop the both of them.

The room was almost in darkness and the few remaining embers glowed fitfully in the grate. She stirred and moved her head against his shoulder. 'We'll have to be going,' he told her. 'It's past eight. That dinner you ordered will be spoilt.'

She turned her softness into him and slipped an arm round his neck. 'There's no rush,' she said. 'The garage haven't phoned about the car yet.'

Marlowe reached for a cigarette and lit it from the silver table lighter that went with the box. As he blew smoke out in a long streamer to the dark ceiling she picked at his shirt with her fingers and said, 'Are you really going to go on defying my uncle?'

'I don't see why not,' he said.

'But you don't stand a chance,' she told him. She slipped an arm around his neck and kissed him. 'I don't want you to get hurt.'

He grinned, his teeth gleaming in the darkness. She struggled up beside him and said, 'What's so funny?'

'That last remark of yours,' he told her. 'You see, I think it's your uncle who's going to end up getting hurt.' He glanced at the luminous dial of his watch and said, 'Round about now Mac must be just leaving for London.'

She switched on a standard lamp and there was incredulity on her face. 'But why is he going to London?'

Marlowe shrugged. 'To sell a truckload of produce at the greatest market in the world, Covent Garden. Even your uncle doesn't cut much ice there.'

For a moment she looked dubious and then she smiled and hugged him. 'Oh, I think it's a wonderful idea. I hope it works for you.' She stood up and stretched and looked at herself in the mirror. She gave a little shriek. 'My goodness, what a sight I look. I must go and change.' She smiled and rumpled his hair. 'Straighten your tie like a good boy and have another drink while I'm getting ready.' As she walked to the door she added, 'I'll phone the garage and see what the delay is.'

Marlowe helped himself to another Martini and listened to the muffled sound of her voice as she used the telephone in the hall. A moment later she opened the door and said, 'They'll deliver it within fifteen minutes. I shan't be long.' She closed the door again and Marlowe picked up a magazine and idly browsed through it.

After a moment or two he tossed it to one side and considered the events of the evening. He didn't try to pretend to himself that he was in love with Jenny O'Connor. There was no need. It was a peculiar type of relationship he had experienced only once before in his life: a tremendous chemistry which gave rise to a physical craving that had to be satisfied.

He checked his watch again. It was almost nine o'clock. By now Mac should be fairly started. He leaned back and stared at the ceiling and tried to calculate the time the Jamaican would arrive in London. Probably about three in the morning. They should see him back by lunchtime easily. One thing was certain. The plan had to succeed. If it didn't it would put Magellan out of business. Of that there was no doubt.

The door clicked open and she entered the room. She was wearing a black, sleeveless knitted dress that was completely form fitting. She smiled and held out a fur coat and he draped it across her shoulders. 'I'm beginning to wonder if I can afford you,' he told her.

She smiled and led the way towards the front door. 'Don't worry about that. I've got plenty of money.'

For a moment some essential core of male pride caused him to feel resentful and then he smiled. After all, why not?

74

It was O'Connor's money. A car horn sounded outside and when she opened the door they found a white-overalled mechanic standing beside the Jaguar. 'You shouldn't have any trouble with it now, Miss O'Connor,' he said cheerfully.

'Thanks, Jerry,' she told him. She turned to Marlowe. 'You can drive if you like.' He handed her in and then went around to the other side and climbed behind the wheel.

The big car handled like a dream; when they reached the main road leading out of Barford, Marlowe accelerated until the needle lifted towards eighty. 'It's a lovely car,' he told her.

She smiled. 'The best. Haven't you ever wanted a car like this?'

For a brief moment he hovered on the brink of telling her about his past. About the days when he'd driven a car like this all the time. When he'd had money and clothes and women. Everything a man could ever want and yet he didn't tell her these things. He didn't tell her because he suddenly realized that things like that had lost their importance. A car was a car, it had an engine and four wheels and it got you from place to place. Was it really so important to have one that cost two thousand pounds?

He cursed silently. If he went on thinking things like that he was going to spoil the evening. Deliberately he pushed them back into some dark corner of his mind and turned into the car park of the road house which they had now reached. As they walked towards the entrance, he forced his mind to concentrate on enjoying the rest of the evening.

It was eleven o'clock when he turned the car into the courtyard outside Jenny O'Connor's flat and stopped the engine. For a moment they sat in silence and then she said, 'I really enjoyed myself. You dance exceptionally well for such a big man.'

He shrugged. 'Give the credit to those Martinis. I wasn't with you half the time.'

She chuckled. 'Coming in for a night-cap?' She placed a warm hand on his arm and something stirred inside him.

After all, why not? He opened the door and started to get out.

A fist lifted into his face and some inexplicable reflex action caused him to duck so that the blow glanced off his cheek. He slammed the door outwards and it thudded against some solid body as he hurled himself forward, ice cold rage surging through him.

A foot tripped him and he hurtled to the cobbles, instinctively putting his hands to his face and rolling away to avoid the swinging kicks. A foot caught him in the side, another grazed his face and then he was on his feet again. Jenny O'Connor hadn't screamed once. For a moment, a terrible suspicion surged through him that perhaps she had played him false and then her front door opened. Light flooded in a golden shaft across the courtyard.

'Inside, Hugh! Inside!' she cried.

In the shaft of light, Blacky Monaghan and his two friends stood revealed. One of them was holding a length of iron railing in both hands and he suddenly darted forward and swung for Marlowe's head. Marlowe ducked and the bar rang against the stone wall behind him. He lifted his foot savagely into the man's crutch. The bar rattled against the cobbles and the man gave a terrible, choking cry and sank to the ground.

Monaghan stood back and wiped a hand across his brow. From the sound of him he'd been drinking. 'That won't do you much good, you bastard,' he snarled. He spoke to his remaining ally without taking his eyes off Marlowe. 'Go get him, Paddy. Slice him up good.'

Paddy took his hand out of his right pocket and slowly opened an old-fashioned bone-handled razor. He started towards Marlowe, his hand extended. Marlowe waited until he was only three or four feet away, then he dropped to one knee, picked up the iron bar his first assailant had dropped and smashed it across Paddy's right arm. The bone snapped like a dry twig. Paddy slipped to the cobbles in a dead faint, his face contorted into a mask of agony.

As Marlowe started to get up from his knee, Monaghan came in with a rush and kicked him in the side, lifting him over and backwards against the wall. The Irishman moved in fast, his foot raised to stamp down on the unprotected face. Marlowe grabbed the foot and twisted and Monaghan fell heavily across him. For several moments they rolled over and over across the cobbles tearing at each other's throats and then, as they crashed into the far wall, Marlowe pulled himself on top. He slammed his fist solidly against the Irishman's jaw twice, and Monaghan's head rolled to one side and he lay still.

Marlowe scrambled to his feet and leaned against the wall for a moment. After a while he turned and walked towards the door. Jenny was standing there looking at him, a strange expression in her eyes. 'My God, can't anyone get the better of you?' she said.

He ignored the remark and pushed her inside. 'You didn't phone the police did you?' She shook her head and he nodded. 'Good! Let me have a double brandy. When I've gone, phone your uncle and tell him what's happened. He'll have to come round to pick his boys up himself.'

She quickly poured brandy and handed him the glass. 'Are they all right?' she said, uncertainty in her voice.

He shrugged. 'That kind are always all right. If you mean have I killed any of them, the answer is no. Your uncle will have to get a doctor though, and the kind of doctor who handles cases like this doesn't come cheap.'

'Blacky Monaghan will kill you next time,' she said with conviction.

Marlowe shrugged and straightened his tie. 'A lot of people have tried to kill me,' he told her. 'I'm still here.'

'Your face is an awful mess,' she said. 'You'd better come into the bathroom and I'll fix it.'

He managed a grin. 'No thanks. O'Connor might have somebody waiting in there for me as well.' He leaned over and brushed her cheek. 'It's been nice, angel, but the party's over for now. I'd better get out of here. Give me five minutes and then phone him.'

As he passed through the courtyard, Paddy was beginning to moan and the third man sobbed steadily like a small child. Marlowe moved rapidly along the dark street. He was lucky. As he emerged into the square, a taxi crossed in front of him and he flagged it down.

He lay back against the upholstered seat and closed his eyes. He was tired, very tired and his body was a mass of bruises. Each time he breathed in, his chest hurt where Monaghan's boot had landed and he wondered if anything was broken. When he considered what had happened he realized that he had been expecting it all night. After all, Monaghan had given him fair warning. He and his friends must have planned the whole thing very carefully.

Marlowe twisted his face into a tired smile. At least he'd kept them busy for the evening while Mac was taking the stuff south. His plan had worked beautifully and he'd got to know Jenny O'Connor very well indeed. Taking it all in all, it had been a profitable evening, kicks and bruises notwithstanding.

He got out of the taxi at the gate and paid the man. For a moment he stood in the darkness listening to the sound of the engine dying away in the distance and then he turned and walked across the yard to the front door.

There was a light on in the kitchen, showing faintly through the crack under the door, and he groped his way towards it and turned the knob. Maria was sitting in an old rocking chair by the kitchen fire crying steadily. She raised a tear-stained face and gave a gasp of horror. 'Oh, Hugh, what have they done to you?'

In a moment she was across the room and in his arms. He held her close as sobs shook her small body and gently smoothed her hair. 'What is it, angel?' he said. 'There's nothing to worry about. They've only chipped the edges a little.'

She raised her face, swollen and puffed up with weeping and said brokenly, 'Mac telephoned through from a little place near Peterborough. He went into a roadside café for a cup of tea and when he came out someone had stolen the truck.' She shook her head helplessly from side to side.

'Don't you see what this means, Hugh? We're finished. There's nothing more we can do.'

As her body was shaken with fresh sobs Marlowe held her close and stared bitterly into space. He decided that if O'Connor had been in the room at that moment he would have killed him with his bare hands.

7

Mac returned in the late afternoon of the following day. Marlowe was working on one of the trucks when he heard the engine. He straightened up and started to wipe his hands on an old rag as Mac drove straight into the barn and came to a halt. He switched off and jumped to the ground.

'So you got the truck back?' Marlowe said as he approached.

The Jamaican shook his head. 'Yes, but the load was missing when the police found it. Man, I feel real bad about this.'

Marlowe offered him a cigarette. 'Don't start blaming yourself. The same thing would have happened to me.'

'How's the old man?' Mac asked.

Marlowe struck a match on the wall and held it out to him. 'Not so good. He's taken it pretty hard, and on top of that his rheumatism's got worse. He's in bed.'

'This is going to break him,' Mac said bitterly. 'The dirty bastards.'

'Never mind about them at the moment,' Marlowe said. 'Tell me what happened.'

Mac spread his hands in a gesture of bewilderment. 'That's the crazy thing. Nothing happened. I'd been driving for about three hours when I came to this transport café near Peterborough. I parked alongside about fifteen other trucks, and went in and had a cup of tea and a sandwich.

When I came out fifteen minutes later, the truck had gone.'

'What did you do then?'

'Got straight on to the local police. The sergeant who handled the case was a nice guy.' Mac laughed shortly. 'He told me it happens every night somewhere along the road.'

Marlowe nodded. 'He's right, it does. That's where O'Connor has been so clever. No hold-up, no coshing, nothing so dramatic. To the police it's just a routine job, and he knows we won't tell them any different.'

Mac nodded and sighed. 'They found the truck at ten o'clock this morning. It was parked up a side road about ten miles from the café.'

Marlowe leaned against the wall, his brow knitted in thought. After a while he said, 'Tell me, Mac, what other interests has O'Connor got besides the fruit-and-vegetable game?'

Mac shrugged. 'He has his own sand quarry. That does pretty well, and there's his haulage contract with the Coal Board. Mainly he does general trucking, I'd say.'

Marlowe shook his head impatiently. 'I don't mean his legitimate interests. What does he do under cover of darkness? Papa Magellan told me he had a pretty bad reputation during the war.'

Mac shook his head. 'I wouldn't know about that. I was only there for five or six weeks.' He frowned and narrowed his eyes. 'I'm pretty sure there's plenty of crooked work going on there, but nobody ever took me into their confidence.'

Marlowe was disappointed. 'That's a pity,' he said. 'I was hoping you might have known something.'

Mac suddenly brightened. 'Hey, wait a minute. There's the garage on the Birmingham road.'

Marlowe was immediately interested. 'On the Birmingham road?' he said. 'That's on the other side of Barford. What goes on there?'

'That's just the trouble,' Mac told him. 'I don't know. But it's something mighty peculiar. Only Monaghan and the hard boys were ever allowed up there. Once or twice they sent me up with messages from O'Connor and they never even let me through the doors.'

Marlowe's eye narrowed and he said softly, 'So they wouldn't let you see inside, eh?' He grinned and clapped the Jamaican on the back. 'I think we'll pay them a little visit this evening, Mac. What do you say?'

Mac grinned. 'Anything to get a crack in at those bastards is okay with me, boy.'

Marlowe grinned. 'That's fine. You'd better come in and have something to eat now.' As they walked towards the house he added, 'Whatever you do, don't tell the old man or Maria where we're going tonight. Especially Maria. Leave any explaining to me.'

Mac looked surprised, but nodded his head. 'Okay, boy, have it any way you want.'

Maria was in the kitchen when they went in. She looked tired and pale, and gave Mac a wan smile. 'I'm sure sorry about what's happened,' Mac told her.

She managed a smile. 'Don't blame yourself. We know it wasn't your fault.'

'Can I see your father?' the Jamaican asked her.

She sighed. 'He's pretty sick at the moment. The doctor's been to give him a check-up. He thinks he's got a touch of the flu. He's running a temperature, anyway.'

She led the way upstairs and cautiously opened the door of the old man's bedroom. He looked about ten years older, and his cheeks were hollow and sunken. From the sound of his heavy breathing he was asleep.

Maria gently closed the door and they went back downstairs. 'He sure doesn't look good,' Mac observed soberly.

'Everything's hit him at once,' Maria said. 'And he's facing ruin. It's a wonder he isn't dead.'

Marlowe felt desperately sorry for her. She gave a little sob and leaned on the table, her head down. He slipped an arm round her waist. 'Now then, angel. This isn't like you. Keep smiling. Mac and I are going to canvass the market gardeners this evening. We'll get another load together, perhaps even two. We'll try for London again tomorrow night.'

She smiled and wiped a tear from her cheek with the back of her hand. 'Yes, you're right, Hugh. I'm just being silly, and that won't help at all.' She squeezed his hand. 'You're so good to me – both of you.' She smiled again. 'I'll get you your meal.'

They started for Barford in one of the trucks just after seven that evening as the sky was beginning to darken. Marlowe purposely avoided the square on their way through the town, and when Mac tapped him on the shoulder he swung the truck on to a piece of waste ground and killed the motor.

It was by now quite dark and the street lamps were strung away through the darkness back towards Barford like yellow beads. The garage was three or four hundred yards farther along the road, and as they approached it a thin rain began to fall.

When they were about fifty yards away Marlowe stopped and said, 'We won't go any closer this way. You never know who's watching. Let's find a way to get round to the back.'

They tried a narrow alley that was lit with a single old-fashioned gas lamp, and stumbled along its uneven paving. It turned sharply to the right after thirty or forty yards, and continued along the rear of the garage. The brick wall was old and crumbling and about nine feet high. Mac looped his hands, and Marlowe used them as a step and scrambled up on to the wall. He reached down his right hand and heaved the Jamaican up beside him. For a little while they sat there, gaining their bearings, and then they dropped down into the yard inside.

There was an old iron fire-escape up to the second floor, and Marlowe cautiously led the way. They paused on the landing, and he tried the knob of the door. It was locked. For a moment he hesitated, and then Mac stretched out to a near-by window. A moment later he gave a grunt of satisfaction. 'It's open,' he said. There was a creak as the sash was raised, and then he climbed over the rail

82

of the fire escape and scrambled in through the window. Marlowe followed him.

They stood in the darkness listening, and Marlowe was conscious of a peculiar smell. He frowned and sniffed experimentally, and then his brow cleared and he pulled Mac close. 'It's whisky,' he said. 'The real stuff. Can you smell it?'

Mac nodded, and led the way cautiously along the corridor. There was a door at the far end with a broken panel in it through which light streamed. He opened it carefully, and the full aroma of the whisky filled their nostrils.

The room was crowded with crates of bottles, and at the far end there were a great many barrels. Marlowe tapped one of them experimentally. 'It's full,' he observed. He moved over to a nearby table and picked up a handful of labels. 'Look at these,' he said. 'All well-known branded names.'

'But what's going on here?' Mac asked in puzzlement.

'It's a racket as old as the hills,' Marlowe told him. 'Cut liquor. They buy whisky in bulk – it may even be quite good stuff – and dilute it with water. Then they bottle it, stick a well known quality label on, and make at least two hundred per cent profit on each bottle.'

Mac frowned. 'But any drinking man can tell if good liquor's been tampered with.'

Marlowe nodded. 'I know, but this stuff is mainly for the night-club trade, and I don't mean high-class establishments either. The sort of places in Soho where the floozies take the suckers and get a percentage.'

Mac looked about him in awe. 'Man, if we sicked the cops on to this lot friend O'Connor would find himself in real trouble.'

Marlowe nodded grimly. 'About five years' worth.' He went to a door in the corner and opened it quietly. After a moment he beckoned Mac over, motioning him to silence.

They were looking into the main part of the garage. It was empty except for one Bedford three-tonner. It looked like a war-surplus job and was still painted a dull shade of khaki green. There seemed to be no one around. Marlowe approached the truck and peered inside. The interior was full of neatly stacked boxes.

He clambered in and Mac followed him. They squatted down and Marlowe took out a pocket-knife and prised up a corner of the cover of one of the boxes. Inside he could just make out the top of a whisky bottle. He grinned and turned to Mac. 'This must be a load waiting to go out.'

Before Mac could reply there was the sound of a door opening and footsteps approaching the truck. Marlowe quickly motioned to him and they crouched down on the floor. They could hear the conversation quite clearly through the canvas canopy.

There were two people standing outside – O'Connor and Kennedy. O'Connor said, 'Here's the address. It's not far from Lime Street, down towards the docks. If you push this crate along you should be there not much after midnight.'

'Hell, Mr O'Connor, I'd have to sprout wings,' Kennedy protested. 'Liverpool's a hell of a long way off.'

O'Connor's voice was cold as ice-water. 'Listen, Kennedy. I'm paying you good money. I want to see some results for a change. You've made a habit of bungling things lately.' His tone became menacing. 'If you don't like working for me we can always make other arrangements.'

'Oh, no, I didn't mean anything like that, Mr O'Connor,' Kennedy hastened to reassure him, and there was fear in his voice.

O'Connor grunted contemptuously. 'Then see you do things right this time,' he said. 'Sid Brown will hand you a paper packet in exchange for this load. There'll be two thousand quid in it. That's a lot of cash. I want to see you and every penny of it back here for breakfast in the morning, and no excuses.'

The door banged, and the whole truck shook as the engine started. A moment later Marlowe heard the rattle of the sliding-doors being rolled back, and then the truck bumped out into the darkness and picked up speed along the main road.

Marlowe settled himself comfortably with his back against the wooden cases, and said to Mac, 'Where did he say we were going? Near Lime Street and not far from the docks?'

The Jamaican's teeth gleamed in the darkness. 'I've never been to Liverpool,' he said. 'I'm quite looking forward to it.'

Marlowe grinned, turned his coat collar up and pulled his cap down over his eyes. 'Better make yourself as comfortable as you can,' he told Mac. 'We're in for a long trip.'

Several times he fell asleep, but always he came awake again as the old truck bumped or swerved over some particularly bad piece of road. Kennedy made quite good time, and on some of the stretches where traffic was light he pushed the Bedford up to sixty.

On the last occasion that he awakened, Marlowe found they were moving through the suburbs of Liverpool, and when he checked his watch he saw that it was just coming up to midnight. He gently nudged Mac, and the Jamaican came awake like a cat. 'We're nearly there,' Marlowe told him. 'Friend Kennedy's certainly pushed this old bus along.'

'What's our next move going to be?' Mac asked.

Marlowe shrugged. 'I don't know. We'll make it up as we go along.'

About fifteen minutes later, they turned into a quiet, dark street and halted. There was complete silence, and in the distance Marlowe could hear the eerie, mournful hooting of the ships out in the Mersey.

There was no immediate sign of activity, and then the door opened and Kennedy jumped down from the cab. They heard his footsteps along the side of the truck, and then he clambered up over the tailboard and shone a torch. Marlowe plucked it from his hand and directed the beam on to him. 'Hallo, Kennedy,' he said. 'Fancy meeting you here.'

There was an expression of ludicrous dismay on Kennedy's face, and he opened his mouth to cry out. Mac hit him with a beautiful short-arm jab in the stomach, and he collapsed across them, gasping for breath. Marlowe stuffed a handkerchief into his mouth and tied his hands with his own belt. Then they pulled several cases out from the back of the pile and pushed him into the space.

They had just dismounted from the truck when two vans appeared from the darkness and parked a few feet away. Four men came forward, and Marlowe leaned against the tailboard of the truck, fists clenched in the darkness in case of trouble.

A small bird-like man grinned and lit a cigarette. 'I'm Sid Brown,' he said. 'You boys from O'Connor?'

'That's right,' Marlowe told him. 'We've got the stuff inside and not a bottle broken.'

Sid Brown nodded. 'New aren't you? I ain't seen you before.'

Marlowe nodded. 'No, we've just started working for O'Connor.'

Sid leered and placed a finger against one side of his nose. 'A good boy, O'Connor,' he said. 'Very wide. You'll do well with him.'

His three assistants were transferring the contents into the two vans at a fantastic speed. 'Doesn't pay to hang around here for long,' Sid said. 'The coppers are too bloody keen for my liking.'

'What about the cash?' Marlowe said. 'If we have to move in a hurry I'd like to take it with me.'

Sid grinned. 'Oh, yes, the old lolly. I was forgetting.' He took a paper packet out of his raincoat and handed it over. 'All in fivers,' he said. 'And they aren't hot.'

Marlowe tore open the packet and examined the money in the light of Kennedy's torch. It was all there. 'You're a cautious one, I must say,' Sid Brown told him in an injured voice. 'You won't find me getting up to any of those tricks. I pay good money for good stuff. Always have done, always will do. It's the only way to get a reputation.'

As his men took the last of the cases out of the truck one of them said, 'Here, what the hell's this?'

Sid moved over to the tailboard and shone a powerful torch on the inanimate form of Kennedy. 'Here, what's going on?' he said. 'Who's that bloke?'

Marlowe grinned and slapped him on the back. 'Don't worry about him,' he said. 'That's my cousin Charlie. He likes to travel that way.'

At the first sign of an alarm Mac had quietly melted into the darkness, and now the truck engine roared into life. Marlowe turned quickly and jumped up into the cab. As he slammed the door he leaned out. 'Nice to have done business with you, Sid. See you again sometime.'

The truck moved forward into the darkness, leaving the astonished Sid and his vans behind.

Mac was laughing so much he could hardly keep the wheel steady. 'Man, is O'Connor going to be sick?'

'Two thousand pounds. All your troubles are over. And he can't go to the police without exposing his whole racket,' Marlowe said. He leaned back and lit a cigarette. 'Yes, I'd call it a very satisfactory night's work.' He looked at his watch. It was almost one o'clock. 'We'll take turns driving,' he said. 'With luck we'll be back by six.'

It rained hard during the next few hours, and it was nearer seven when they turned the truck on to the waste ground near the garage and halted beside their own.

When Marlowe climbed into the back of the Bedford he found that Kennedy had managed to get rid of the bandage. As he bent down to untie him, Kennedy said, 'You'll never get away with this.'

Marlowe dragged him to his feet and half threw him over the tailboard. 'What are you going to do?' he jeered. 'Go to the police and tell them you had a cargo of cut whisky hijacked? I should imagine they'd be very interested.'

Kennedy was almost crying. 'For God's sake, Marlowe, what am I going to do? O'Connor will kill me if I go back to him now.'

He seemed near to breaking point. Marlowe stood looking at him, and something like pity moved inside him. 'If you've got any sense you won't go back to him,' he said. 'You'll get to hell out of here as fast as you can.'

He took the packet of fivers from his pocket and extracted ten. 'There's fifty quid,' he said, handing the money to Kennedy. 'The London express leaves in an hour.'

He ignored the mumbled words of thanks and pulled himself up into the cab of their own truck beside Mac, who was sitting behind the wheel with the engine ticking over. 'That was a pretty decent thing to do, man,' the Jamaican said as they moved away.

Marlowe shrugged. 'Mugs like Kennedy shouldn't be allowed out on their own.' He rested his head in the corner and closed his eyes, effectively cutting off any further attempts at conversation.

When they rolled into the farmyard half an hour later, Maria was in the act of walking towards the barn. She ran forward as Marlowe jumped to the ground. 'Where have you been?' she demanded. 'I've been worried sick.'

He ignored her question. 'How's your father?' he said.

'Much better this morning,' she told him. 'He's sitting up in bed asking for you. I didn't know what to tell him.'

She led the way indoors and they followed her upstairs to the old man's room. Papa Magellan was sitting up in bed with a woollen scarf around his neck. His half-finished breakfast was on a tray in front of him. His face lit up as Marlowe appeared in the doorway. 'Hugh, where have you been, boy? What have you been up to?' he demanded.

'They won't tell me anything,' Maria said.

Mac leaned against the door, and Marlowe unbuttoned his coat and took out the packet of five-pound notes. 'Your troubles are over, Papa,' he said, and tossed the packet on to the bed. 'There's two thousand quid in there.'

Maria gasped and put a hand to her throat, and her face went bone white. 'Hugh, what have you done?' she said fearfully.

The old man's face was puzzled. 'Where did this money come from?'

Marlowe shrugged. 'From O'Connor. We found out he runs a racket in cut liquor. Last night we delivered one of his loads for him in Liverpool. All the customer was interested in was getting the whisky. He gave us the money without a murmur.' He grinned. 'So there you are, Papa. No more troubles.'

The old man's face was stern. He said to the girl, 'Maria, bring me one of the large manila envelopes from the drawer over there.'

Maria did as she was told and handed him the envelope silently. 'Now give me a pen and some stamps,' he told her. Marlowe watched silently as the old man counted thirty notes out of the pile and put them on one side. 'I've taken a hundred and twenty pounds,' he said. 'That's what I reckon that load would have brought in London.'

Marlowe was amazed. 'You mean you're sending the rest of it back to O'Connor?' he cried. 'That's crazy.'

Papa Magellan shook his head. 'It's good sense. This is dirty money, wrongly come by. I've taken what I reckon O'Connor owes me. No more, no less.' He finished addressing the envelope and carefully stuck down the flap. When he had affixed the stamps he held the envelope out to Marlowe. 'I want you to post this.' For a moment Marlowe hesitated, and the old man said, 'Post it now.'

Marlowe sighed and took the envelope. 'All right, Papa. Have it your own way.'

He left the room without another word and went downstairs. The post box was several hundred yards down the road. It was an old-fashioned, rectangular box set in a rough stone wall with Queen Victoria's initials still engraved on it in wrought iron.

He stood in front of the box and hesitated for a moment, and then he slipped the letter into his inside breast pocket and retraced his steps to the house.

When he reached the gate Mac was leaning against the wall. There was a sombre expression on his face, and he said, 'You didn't post it, did you?'

Marlowe shook his head. 'No, it would have been a stupid thing to do.'

Mac sighed. 'I sure hope you know what you're doing, man,' he said, and followed Marlowe into the house.

Maria was in the kitchen cooking breakfast. When he entered the room she turned, an eager smile on her face, and said, 'You've posted it?'

Marlowe forced a smile to his lips. 'Yes, much against my better judgement.'

A radiant smile blossomed on her face. 'Oh, I'm so glad, Hugh. Papa was right, you know.'

She turned back to the stove and Marlowe sat down at the table, rage in his heart. He knew what he was doing all right. He wasn't going to throw good money away because of an old man's whim. He knew what he was doing, and yet he ground his nails into the palms of his hands in impotent rage because she believed him when he had lied to her.

8

Marlowe made the rounds of the market gardeners that afternoon and paid them off. When he drove back into the barn Maria was sitting on the table, swinging her legs and talking to Mac, who was working on the engine of one of the trucks. As Marlowe climbed down she poured coffee into a cup and offered it to him. 'You're just in time.'

He drank some of the coffee gratefully. 'That's good. It's turning pretty cold outside now.'

'How did you get on with the growers?' she asked.

He shrugged. 'No trouble there at the moment. They all got their money, so they were pretty satisfied.' He nodded towards the truck. 'I've got a hell of a load on this time. Apples and pears, some tomatoes, and quite a few plums.'

He gave her the list and she nodded in satisfaction. 'That's good. There's a steady demand for all these things in the main London markets. I checked in the morning paper.'

Marlowe turned to Mac with a grin. 'You should have no difficulty in getting rid of this lot when you get there.'

Before the Jamaican could reply Maria said quickly, 'But surely you'll go with him, Hugh? It will obviously be so much safer with two of you.'

Marlowe shook his head and clapped Mac on the shoulder. 'He doesn't need me.'

Mac grinned good naturedly. 'You'd only be in the way, man.'

'It's not fair, Hugh,' Maria stormed. 'Why should Mac have to do it on his own?' There was an expression of anger on her face. 'I think you should go with him.'

Marlowe choked back an angry retort and managed to keep his voice steady. 'Listen, angel, I don't give a damn what you think. I'm not going to London. I've got my reasons, and they aren't any of your business.'

Her face was white and two red spots flared in her cheeks. As she opened her mouth to reply he turned abruptly and walked out of the barn across the yard towards the house.

When he entered Papa Magellan's room the old man was sitting up reading a newspaper. He looked over the top of his reading-glasses and said, 'You look pretty mad, son. What's the trouble?'

Marlowe lit a cigarette and paced up and down the room. 'It's your damned daughter,' he said. 'She's getting all steamed up again because I'm sending Mac to London.'

The old man nodded. 'And being a woman she wants to know why you can't go?'

Marlowe sighed and sat down in a chair. 'Why the hell can't she take a hint, like you and Mac have done, and mind her own business?'

Magellan smiled. 'Open that cupboard, son. There's an album on the top shelf.' Marlowe did as he was asked and handed him the old-fashioned red-morocco photograph album. 'Have a look at this,' Magellan said, opening the album to a certain page.

Marlowe twisted the album round so that he could see properly. For a moment he thought he was looking at Maria. 'Is this her mother?' he asked.

Papa Magellan nodded. 'Yes, that was my Maria. As you can see they are like peas in a pod.' He smiled gently and closed the book. 'Not only in looks. I'm afraid that by nature my wife thirsted after knowledge, very much as Maria does.' He shrugged and handed the album back to Marlowe. 'It's a fault common to most women.'

Marlowe got up and put the album back on the shelf. As he was about to close the door he noticed a shotgun leaning in a corner of the cupboard, partially obscured by hanging clothes. He took it out and examined it closely. It was a double-barrelled twelve-bore, beautifully polished and engraved. He whistled softly. 'This must have cost you a pound or two.'

Papa Magellan smiled faintly. 'Yes, I like the feel of a good gun. There was a time when I was fond of an early morning tramp over the fields, and a try at a pigeon or two, but I'm past it now.' He leaned forward and tried to see into the cupboard. 'There should be a box of cartridges on that shelf somewhere.'

Marlowe found them with no difficulty. 'Yes, they're here.'

'Good!' Papa Magellan said. 'Then take the gun. You and Mac can have a little relaxation in the fields at the back.'

Marlowe grinned. 'We can always pretend we're blasting away at O'Connor.'

He examined the gun with real pleasure and there was a short silence that was broken by the old man. 'Maria is in love with you, isn't she?'

Marlowe looked up slowly. For a moment he hesitated and then he shrugged. 'Yes, I suppose she is.'

The old man nodded. 'From the beginning it was obvious to me.' He smiled gently and went on, 'Are you in love with her?'

Marlowe laughed harshly. 'Papa, I'm not in love with anyone. I've got other things to worry about.' He shook his head and got up. 'I don't want to be tied down. I can't afford it.'

The old man nodded, his eyes clouding over a little. 'Then it will be better if you go soon. Maria will suffer a great deal over this.'

Marlowe sighed and nodded. 'I'm sorry about that, Papa, but you needn't worry. I'll be moving on very soon anyway. Perhaps in another week. If things work out all right we should have O'Connor straightened out by then and when I leave you'll still have Mac. He's a good man.'

Magellan nodded and smiled faintly. 'So are you, son. Don't rate yourself too low.' He coughed several times and lay back against the pillow. 'This trouble you are in that keeps you from going to London? Is it bad trouble?'

Marlowe paused at the door, the shotgun under one arm and shook his head. 'A few old friends who want to see me and I don't want to see them,' he said. 'Nothing I can't handle.'

The old man nodded and smiled and his eyes half closed. 'Good,' he said. 'I am pleased. Now I think I will sleep.' Marlowe gently closed the door and went downstairs.

During the remainder of the afternoon Maria made a point of avoiding him. When he and the Jamaican were having their evening meal she addressed herself to Mac only and completely ignored Marlowe. At first he was faintly amused by her attitude, but after a while he was conscious of a slight feeling of resentment that increased as the evening wore on.

He and Mac spent several hours checking the engine of the truck that was to make the London trip and packed the boxes and skips containing the produce with infinite care. Marlowe left the Jamaican to make one or two last minute preparations and walked through the darkness towards the house.

Maria was sitting by the kitchen fire reading a magazine. 'Mac's almost ready to move,' he told her. 'I'll take the thermos flask and sandwiches to him if you like.'

'I can manage myself, thank you,' she replied frostily, getting up from her chair.

Marlowe shrugged and went back along the corridor to the front door. He stood in the porch for a moment, breathing in the cold night air and suddenly there was a crash of glass as something hurtled out through the window of the barn.

Marlowe started to run and behind him he heard Maria call out in fear. As he approached the barn three figures ran out through the lighted doorway and disappeared into the dark. He paused for a moment and glanced hurriedly inside. Mac was sprawled out on the floor by the truck. Even as Marlowe hesitated, the sudden roar of a motor shattered the stillness nearby. A moment later it was dwindling into the distance.

He ran forward into the barn and knelt down by the Jamaican. There was a trickle of blood down one temple and when his fingers gently explored the scalp they encountered a fast rising bump.

Maria dropped on her knees beside him. 'Is he all right?' she demanded, anxiously.

Marlowe nodded. 'Just a nasty knock on the head.' He lifted the Jamaican in his arms and walked out of the barn back towards the house. He kicked open the door of the living-room and placed his burden on the old-fashioned settee.

Maria dropped on her knees beside him with a damp cloth and gently washed away the blood. After a moment Mac groaned and opened his eyes. 'Hallo there, man,' he said to Marlowe. 'Somebody sure cracked down on my skull.'

Marlowe nodded. 'What happened?' he demanded.

Mac tried to sit up and Maria gently pushed him down. 'I was tightening a nut on the engine cowling when I heard a footfall behind me,' he said. 'As I turned round someone swung at me. I figured it was the trucks they were after so I hurled the spanner I was holding through the window.'

'That was a bright idea,' Marlowe told him. 'It frightened them off before they could do any damage.'

Mac tried to get up again. 'I'll have to be moving,' he said.

Marlowe pushed him down. 'Nothing doing. You couldn't drive five miles in your present state.'

He moved towards the door and Mac said, 'But what are we going to do?'

Marlowe grinned. 'I'll have to go for you.' As Mac started to protest, he added, 'It's the only possible thing. Don't worry. Nobody's going to stop me getting there.'

He crossed the yard to the barn and went inside. He opened one of the tool cupboards at the back of the workbench and took out the shotgun. He broke it and examined the barrels. They were in perfect condition. He tore open the box of cartridges and loaded the weapon, then he put a handful of cartridges into one of his pockets and replaced the box in the cupboard.

As he walked back to the truck, Maria came in carrying a thermos flask and a tin containing sandwiches. She paled at the sight of the gun. 'What are you going to do with that?' she demanded.

He opened the door of the cab and placed the shotgun along the rear of the bench seat. 'That's my ace-in-the-hole,' he said. 'If they try any funny business this trip they'll find they've made a big mistake.'

She shook her head. 'Guns are bad business,' she told him. 'When you start that sort of thing who knows where it will end?'

He took the coffee and sandwiches from her and stowed them under the seat. 'Don't worry,' he said gently. 'I'm not going to kill anybody. I won't need to. It's amazing how quickly the average thug deflates when he finds himself looking down the barrel of a gun.'

He smiled reassuringly and patted her cheek and then he climbed up behind the wheel and started the engine. As he eased off the handbrake she ran forward and said desperately, 'I'm sorry, Hugh. I'm sorry for the way I've treated you today.'

'That's all right, angel,' he said and pressed his foot on the accelerator. The roar of the engine filled the barn and he was unable to hear the next thing she said. Her mouth worked desperately and he nodded and smiled and took the truck forward out into the darkness.

As he dropped down the hill into Litton he wondered what she had been trying to say to him and he remembered Papa Magellan's words and sighed. Perhaps things were working out for the best after all. Perhaps it would be a good idea if he took advantage of this trip to London to wrap up his own business. Afterwards he could leave the Magellans and their problems far behind. He had done enough.

He reached inside his shirt and pulled out the length of string which hung around his neck. On the end of it was the key to the safe deposit box. He slipped the key back inside his shirt and a feeling of elation swept through him. Yes, everything was happening for the best after all. The safe deposit firm probably opened at nine or nine-thirty. He could be driving out of London again by ten o'clock. He lit a cigarette and leaned back comfortably in the seat.

After he had been driving for about an hour it began to rain. He cursed softly and switched on the windscreen wipers. He turned on all his headlights and settled back again into his seat. At that moment the truck lifted over a small hill and the powerful beam of his headlights picked out a green Jaguar parked about thirty or forty yards along the road. A figure stood at the side of the car flagging him down.

Marlowe grinned savagely and started to depress the accelerator and then he frowned and slammed his foot hard against the hydraulic brake. The truck skidded to a halt and he cut the engine and looked down into the pale, rain-soaked face of Jenny O'Connor.

'What on earth are you doing here?' he demanded.

She seemed to have difficulty in speaking and there was desperation in her eyes. There was complete silence except for the rain drumming hard against the canopy of the truck and Marlowe smiled and reached for the shotgun as the dark shadows rose from behind the Jaguar and moved forward.

Monaghan pulled the girl out of the way and reached for the door handle. 'Right, you bastard,' he said. 'This is where you get yours.'

Marlowe pushed the double barrels of the shotgun out through the window. An expression of complete fury appeared on Monaghan's face. 'You wouldn't dare,' he snarled.

'Wouldn't I?' Marlowe said gently and he thumbed back the hammers.

The other three men were strangers to him, but they bore the mark of hired bullies. One of them said savagely, 'Here, you didn't tell us it was going to be like this.'

Marlowe raised the gun very deliberately and pointed it at them. 'Maybe you haven't heard about a shotgun and what it can do. I'll tell you. It spreads. If I fire it now all three of you'll get it right in the face. If anyone's kicking after that I still have another barrel.'

The three men moved back hurriedly and Jenny clutched at the window and said desperately: 'They made me come, Hugh. They knew you would stop for me. It was my uncle who forced me to come.'

She started to cry bitterly, the tears coursing down her face and mingling with the rain and Marlowe said, 'Go round to the other door and get in. You told me you could drive a truck. Now you can show me how good you are.'

As Monaghan opened his mouth, she darted round to the far side of the cab, wrenched open the door, and scrambled up behind the wheel. In a moment the engine roared and she moved into gear as competently as any truck driver Marlowe had ever seen.

Monaghan gave a roar of rage and reached for the door handle. Marlowe rammed the barrel into the Irishman's stomach. As the truck moved away he looked back and saw Monaghan huddled over in the road, his three bravos standing around him.

As he stowed the shotgun behind the seat he said, 'How did they know I'd be going to London tonight?'

She spoke without turning her head, her eyes concentrating on the road ahead. 'My uncle sent someone round to buy produce from some of the market gardeners Mr Magellan deals with. He found out that you'd been round already today and guessed you'd be trying for London again.'

Marlowe grunted and lit a cigarette. 'Somebody paid us a call tonight and laid Mac out cold. Who was it? Monaghan and his pals?'

She nodded and glanced briefly across at him. 'I was outside in the lane in the car with my uncle. They meant to put your trucks out of commission, but you arrived on the scene too quickly.'

'They seem to be using you quite a lot at the moment,' he said.

She turned the heavy truck into a difficult bend with the skill of a racing driver. 'My uncle doesn't trust me any more. He was furious about what happened the other night. Monaghan's two friends are still in bed. One of them has a broken arm.'

'Who were those characters he had with him tonight?' Marlowe asked.

'They arrived from Birmingham this afternoon.' She shuddered. 'Revolting men. My uncle forced me to go with them. They thought you would stop when you saw me and my car.'

He reached for the thermos and poured himself a cup of coffee. 'Well, their little scheme didn't work. Thanks to my ace-in-the-hole.' As he put the flask back under the seat he added, 'You can pull up now and I'll take over.'

When they had halted she sat silently at the wheel for a moment. After a while she turned and said, with something like horror in her voice, 'You wouldn't have used that gun, would you?'

Marlowe looked surprised. 'What the hell do you think I brought it for?' He laughed harshly. 'Don't start telling me it isn't proper behaviour. I suppose you'd have preferred to stand by and watch Monaghan and his pals use me as a football?'

She sighed. 'No, I suppose you're right in a way.'

She slid from behind the wheel. As he moved over and took her place he said, 'I'm damned sure I'm right. With a certain kind of man you have to use the first thing that comes to hand and Monaghan's that kind.'

He rested his hands on the wheel. 'Well, next stop London as far as I'm concerned. You can come all the way or I'll drop you off at the first big town if you like.'

'I'll come all the way if you don't mind.' She leaned back into the darkness of the corner and as he reached for the starter said, 'Hugh, you don't love me, do you?'

He turned and looked straight at her. 'I don't love anyone.'

She nodded. 'Yes, I thought so.'

'Do you still want to go all the way?' he demanded.

He couldn't see her face in the darkness but she answered in a steady voice, 'Yes, I'll still go all the way with you.' He pulled the starter and a moment later they were moving again.

It was almost seven-thirty when they reached Covent Garden due to carburettor trouble on the way which had taken Marlowe over an hour to diagnose and put right. The main rush of the day was already over at the great market, but to his surprise, Marlowe found no difficulty in disposing of his entire load. The first wholesaler he tried came straight out, examined his load and gave him a cheque for one hundred and sixty pounds on the spot. What was even better, he asked for another load of the same quality to be delivered on the following day.

Jenny O'Connor looked surprisingly well considering the way in which she had spent the night. Her skirt was of such excellent material that it had creased little and she produced a ribbon from a pocket of her suede jacket and tied her flaxen hair in a pony tail.

'Even by London standards you look pretty good,' Marlowe assured her as he stopped the truck on Shaftesbury Avenue, not far from Piccadilly.

She smiled. 'I don't know about that, but it makes me feel better, anyway.'

He offered her a cigarette. 'What are you going to do? Come back with me?'

She shook her head and said slowly, 'No, I don't think so. I'll return by train. I want to take my time. I've got a lot to think over in view of what's happened.'

'Are you all right for money?' he said.

She smiled and laid a hand on his arm. 'Yes, I've got plenty. I may even decide to stay for a couple of days.'

At that moment Marlowe glanced casually through the windscreen at a black limousine which had pulled into the kerb a few yards in front of the truck. There was something vaguely familiar about it. The door opened and Faulkner, dapper and correct in an elegant grey flannel suit and Homburg hat, got out and turned to speak to someone who was still in the car.

Marlowe ducked rapidly, a hand to his face and Jenny said, 'What is it, Hugh? What's the matter?'

'That man standing by the limousine,' he told her. 'An old acquaintance I'd prefer not to meet.'

Faulkner straightened up and the limousine moved away from the kerb. He seemed to look directly at the truck and then he turned and crossing the pavement, entered a restaurant.

Jenny O'Connor squeezed Marlowe's arm. 'You can look up now. He's gone into that restaurant.' She opened the door, jumped down to the ground and said urgently, 'Go on, Hugh. Get moving.' She merged into the crowd and he moved into the main traffic stream. He looked back once and caught a glimpse of her flaxen hair and then she was gone.

His business at the safe deposit took him precisely ten minutes. They opened for business at nine-thirty and he was waiting on the doorstep, key in hand. As the clerk opened the small safe he said pleasantly, 'It's been a long time since you last called, sir.'

Marlowe smiled. 'Yes, I've been out of the country.'

Inwardly his stomach was churning and as the clerk talked, his words became a meaningless mumble. The safe door opened and he took out the shabby, old-fashioned Gladstone bag. He was still talking as they went upstairs, but Marlowe didn't hear a word.

Outside the pavement seemed to move beneath his feet and the bright, early morning sun dazzled him. The truck was parked in a side street and he almost ran towards it. He scrambled up into the cab and slammed the door. He placed the Gladstone bag on the seat beside him and lit a cigarette with trembling hands.

For a long time he just looked at the bag and he was conscious of sweat trickling down from his armpits and of a sudden dryness in the throat. With a muffled curse, he reached for the bag and wrenched it open.

The money was there, all in neat little bundles, most of it as crisp and clean as the day it had been drawn from the bank. For a moment or two he looked at it. Twenty thousand pounds, he thought, and it's all mine. I sweated for it and I earned it. Every penny of it.

He closed the bag and pushed it under the seat. A moment later the truck was moving northwards through the main traffic stream and he was grinning all over his face like a little boy.

9

The truck lurched across the cobbles of the farmyard and rolled to a halt inside the barn. Marlowe switched off the engine and checked the time. It was almost two o'clock.

He pulled the Gladstone bag from beneath the seat and jumped down to the ground. For several moments he stood, weighing the bag in one hand, his eyes searching the barn for a suitable hiding place. At the far end of the building a rickety ladder lifted to a loft and he walked towards it, eyeing it speculatively.

The ladder creaked and swayed as he mounted it. He paused at the top and surveyed the loft. It was crammed with the accumulated junk of years. A smile crossed his face and he put the Gladstone bag down beside several old suitcases and pulled the corner of a decaying cricket net half over it. The Gladstone bag looked perfectly at home and he climbed back down the ladder, satisfied.

He paused in the entrance of the barn to light a cigarette. The farm rested quietly in the damp warmth of the afternoon and he saw no sign of anyone as he approached the house.

There was a fire on in the kitchen and the table was laid for one. On the plate he found a hastily scribbled note from Maria telling him his dinner was in the oven and that she and Mac had gone to pick up another load of produce.

Marlowe grinned, screwed the note into a ball and flicked it into the fire. He left the kitchen and went up the back stairs. He opened the door to Papa Magellan's room cautiously and peered in. The old man was propped up against the pillows reading a book. He turned quickly, a smile of welcome on his face. 'Come in, son. Come and tell me what happened.'

Marlowe closed the door and sat on the end of the bed. He took the cheque he had received from the Covent Garden wholesaler and flipped it across to the old man. 'That's what happened,' he said.

The old man examined the cheque incredulously and pursed his lips in a soundless whistle. 'A hundred and sixty pounds. That's wonderful.'

'That's not all,' Marlowe told him. 'They want another load for tomorrow morning.'

Magellan started to laugh and then he broke into a paroxysm of coughing. When he finally managed to catch his breath, he wiped tears from his eyes and said weakly, 'I feel a hundred per cent better already. I'd like to have O'Connor in front of me right now so that I could wave this cheque in his fat face.'

There was the sound of a car entering the yard. Marlowe went to the window and peered out as a large black saloon pulled up. After a second or two the door opened and O'Connor clambered out.

'Who is it?' asked Papa Magellan.

Marlowe frowned. 'You're about to have your wish granted.'

The old man looked bewildered. 'O'Connor?' he said. 'But what on earth can he want here?'

Marlowe shrugged. 'Perhaps he wants to make a deal. I'd better go and find out anyway.'

When he opened the porch door O'Connor was standing with his back to him looking out across the farmyard to the greenhouses and the fields beyond. He turned slowly and took a cigar from his mouth. 'It's a nice piece of property,' he said. 'Very nice indeed.'

'We think so,' Marlowe told him.

For a few moments they challenged each other and then the fat man's face creased into a smile. 'Aren't you going to ask me in?'

Marlowe shrugged and stood to one side. 'Why not?' he said. 'We can always disinfect the place afterwards.'

O'Connor's smile faded, but he forced it back into place. 'Where's the old man? He's the one I've come to see. Not the hired help.'

Marlowe took a single step forward and the fat man backed hurriedly away. 'I don't want any trouble,' he gabbled in a frightened voice. 'I just want to make a straight business proposition to the old man.'

Marlowe looked him over coldly. 'I don't like you, O'Connor,' he said. 'It wouldn't take much to make me break your fat neck. Remember that.'

He turned abruptly and led the way upstairs. When he opened the door to Magellan's room the old man was waiting impatiently, an extra pillow behind him, his back as straight and unyielding as an iron bar.

O'Connor came into the room breathing heavily and flopped down into the chair by the window. It creaked ominously and he took out a handkerchief and ran it over his face. He seemed to find difficulty in breathing and fanned himself vigorously with his hat. After several moments he said, 'My heart isn't what it used to be.' He gulped and ran the handkerchief over his face again. 'Those stairs are damned steep.'

Papa Magellan said in a voice of iron, 'You won't get any sympathy here. Say what you've come to say and get out.'

O'Connor's smile slipped. 'All right,' he said. 'I'll come straight to the point. You're in my way, Magellan. I want you out of here. I'll give you three thousand pounds for this place, trucks included, and I'll settle your mortgage as well. You wouldn't get half that price on the open market and you know it.'

Papa Magellan adjusted his spectacles and picked up his newspaper. 'I'm not interested.'

There was another moment of silence and then O'Connor exploded. 'You damned old fool, you've got to accept. You'll be ruined otherwise.'

The old man looked at Marlowe, an expression of distaste on his face. 'Get him out of here, Hugh,' he said. 'The place is beginning to smell bad.'

O'Connor lurched to his feet and moved forward. 'I'm warning you,' he said threateningly. 'This is your last chance. After this I'll run you off the roads and I won't be too particular how I do it.'

Marlowe gripped him firmly by the arm and propelled him towards the door. Papa Magellan put down his paper and removed his spectacles. 'Just a minute, Hugh.'

Marlowe stopped in the doorway, his hand still gripping O'Connor's arm and the old man said, 'I've known you a long time, O'Connor. We've stood each other more drinks than I can remember. I never approved of some of the ways you made your money, but that didn't mean I disliked you.'

O'Connor tried to pull away and Marlowe tightened his grip painfully. 'Keep still,' he said threateningly.

'I don't know what happened to you,' Papa Magellan continued, 'but during the past year you've turned into a wild beast. Anyone who gets in your way you destroy.' He shook his head and spoke very deliberately. 'Well, I give you fair warning. I've had enough. If you harm anyone or anything belonging to me from now on, I'll seek you out and destroy you for the mad dog that you are.'

He turned back to his newspaper, his hands trembling slightly, and Marlowe pushed O'Connor through the door and along the corridor.

O'Connor seemed to have difficulty in negotiating the stairs and when they reached the bottom he suddenly

104

clutched at the wall, gasping for air, one hand tearing at his collar.

The attack was obviously genuine. Marlowe pushed him down into a chair and loosened his tie and collar. O'Connor's face had turned purple and his lips assumed a peculiar bluish tinge. Marlowe went quickly into the living-room and returned with a glass of brandy.

O'Connor gulped at it greedily and brandy trickled down his chin and soaked into his shirt front. After a few moments his breathing was easier. He smiled weakly up at Marlowe. 'One of these days I'll have one too many of these attacks.'

Marlowe nodded soberly. 'You're carrying too much weight around. It's a wonder your heart's lasted out this long.'

O'Connor struggled to his feet. 'When I was younger I was just like you, son. Big and strong as an ox. Then something went wrong with my glands.' He grinned and coughed several times into his handkerchief. When he looked up moisture streamed from his eyes. 'It's a vale of tears,' he wheezed. 'You never know what's going to happen next.'

Marlowe laughed coldly. 'My heart bleeds for you.'

He took O'Connor by the arm and helped him out to the car and the fat man leaned heavily on him, every step an effort.

When he was safely seated behind the wheel, Marlowe slammed the car door and said, 'I don't want to see your face round here again.'

O'Connor pressed the starter and leaned out of the window. 'You tell the old man to think it over,' he said. 'I'll give him until tonight. I'll be at the warehouse till nine. He can phone me there.'

Before Marlowe could reply his car moved rapidly away across the farmyard in a burst of speed, swerving dangerously as it went through the gate, narrowly avoiding a collision with the Bedford which was about to enter.

Mac halted the truck beside Marlowe and leaned out of the window. 'Hey there, man,' he said. 'It's good to see you. How did it go?'

Marlowe raised a thumb. 'Perfect. I'd no difficulty in getting rid of the stuff at all. In fact, I've promised another load for tomorrow.'

Maria had jumped down from the other side of the cab and she came round, a smile of welcome on her face. 'Was it really a success, Hugh?' she said excitedly.

Marlowe nodded. 'A hundred and sixty quid I got,' he told her. 'As long as we can make up a full load each time, there'll be no difficulty in making it pay.'

'Who was that crazy guy who just left in the saloon?' Mac demanded.

Marlowe grinned. 'No less a person than Mr O'Connor himself.'

An expression of alarm crossed Maria's face. 'What did he want, Hugh? Has there been any trouble?'

Marlowe shook his head. 'There's nothing to worry about. He was here on business. He offered to buy your father out again, but the old man wasn't interested.'

She looked puzzled. 'But what made him try again, I wonder? Papa told him very definitely last time that nothing would make him sell.'

'Yes, but things have changed some since then,' Mac put in. 'We've got him on the run now. And what's more, he knows it.'

The girl turned to Marlowe. 'Do you think that's it, Hugh?' she demanded.

Marlowe nodded reassuringly. 'That's about the size of it, angel. There's nothing to worry about. You go on up to your father and Mac and I will see to this load.'

She smiled in relief and went into the house. Marlowe went round to the other side of the truck and climbed up beside Mac and they drove down into the barn.

'Did you have any trouble on the way?' Mac asked when he had switched off the engine.

Marlowe lit a cigarette and nodded. 'Plenty,' he said and gave the Jamaican a quick summary of the events of the previous night.

When he had finished Mac whistled softly. 'Man, it was a good thing you took that shotgun along.'

106

Marlowe nodded. 'You're telling me.'

They climbed down from the cab and Mac said, 'Do you think they'll try anything tonight?'

'I don't know,' Marlowe frowned. 'I still can't quite understand why O'Connor turned up here today. It doesn't fit.' He grinned and slapped the Jamaican on the shoulder. 'Anyway, not to worry. You can take the shotgun along, just in case.' He shook his head. 'Somehow I don't think you'll need it.'

Mac nodded and said feelingly, 'I hope not.' As they walked round to the back of the truck he added, 'I'd sure like to know how Miss Jenny's getting on. I hate to think of her being mixed up with that mob.'

Marlowe frowned slightly. 'That's one thing I can't understand,' he said. 'O'Connor must be anxious to know what's happened to her and yet he never mentioned it to me.'

Mac considered the point for a moment. 'Perhaps she phoned through from London this morning and told him she wasn't coming back. I can't see her having anything more to do with him after the way she's been treated.'

'I wish I could be as sure,' Marlowe said and lowered the tailboard of the truck.

He yawned and closed his eyes momentarily as a tremendous wave of tiredness enveloped him. Mac put a hand gently on his shoulder. 'Why don't you go in and have a few hours' sleep. You sure could use some.' Marlowe started to protest and Mac gave him a push towards the door. 'Go on, boy, I can manage this lot on my own.'

He found it an effort to mount the stairs and when he passed along the corridor he could hear the murmur of voices from Papa Magellan's room as Maria talked to her father. For a moment he paused, undecided whether to go in or not, and then he went on to the far end of the corridor and opened the door of his own room.

He pulled off his jacket and sat wearily down on the edge of the bed and removed his shoes. He started to unbutton his shirt, but suddenly the effort seemed too great and he fell backwards. As his head struck the pillow he dived head

107

first into darkness.

He came awake to find a hand on his shoulder. Mac was leaning over him, warmly dressed in a jeep coat with a woollen scarf round his neck and gloves on his hands. Marlowe sat up with a start and looked at his watch. It was almost seven-thirty and outside the sky was darkening rapidly.

'Why on earth didn't you wake me?' he said as he swung his legs to the floor.

Mac grinned. 'There wasn't any need, man. I managed to do most of the loading on my own and that old guy Dobie who works in the greenhouses, turned up to help me finish.' He smacked one gloved hand against another. 'Well, I'm raring to go. If anyone gets in my way tonight I'll roll straight over them.'

Marlowe pulled on his shoes and stood up. 'That's the style,' he said. 'Have you got the shotgun in the cab?' Mac nodded and Marlowe went on: 'Good, it gives you some kind of insurance, but don't stop for anything or anybody.'

Mac grinned and slapped him on the shoulder. 'Don't worry about me, man. Nothing's going to stop me this time.'

They went downstairs and out into the yard where the truck stood waiting. A chill breeze was blowing carrying a hint of rain with it and Marlowe shivered. 'It looks like being a murky night.'

Maria appeared from behind him, the thermos flask and a packet of sandwiches in her hand. 'Be careful,' she urged Mac as she handed them up to him.

He grinned down at them and revved up the engine. 'Don't you worry about me, Miss Maria. I feel really lucky tonight. Just like I used to feel before a big fight.'

He waved once and the truck lurched away across the yard, paused for a moment at the gate, and moved into the darkness, its red tail light growing smaller and smaller until it disappeared.

Maria sighed as she turned to go back into the house and Marlowe said, 'Don't worry, angel. He'll be all right this time.'

'I hope so,' she said. The telephone started to ring from

the living-room and she went to answer it. After a few moments she returned, annoyance on her face. 'It's for you.'

Marlowe was surprised. 'Who is it?'

'Find out for yourself.' Maria tossed her head and disappeared into the kitchen, banging the door.

As Marlowe approached the telephone he could hear a voice calling anxiously. He picked up the receiver. 'Hugh Marlowe here. Who's speaking?'

'Hugh, is that you? Thank God you're still there.' It was Jenny O'Connor and she sounded frightened.

'So you decided to return after all,' Marlowe said. 'I hoped you'd have more sense.'

'Never mind that now.' She was almost sobbing. 'I must see you. Can you come to the flat?'

He frowned. 'I'm rather busy at the moment.'

'Please, Hugh, I'm in terrible trouble. You must help me.' There was desperation in her voice.

For a moment he hesitated and then he sighed. 'All right. Where are you.'

'At the flat,' she said. 'How soon can I expect you?'

He glanced at his watch. 'About eight-thirty.' She started to say something else and he cut her short. 'You can tell me when I get there,' he said and replaced the receiver.

He went up to the bedroom for his jacket and a scarf. When he came downstairs Maria was standing in the hall, drying her hands on her apron. 'Well, what did she want?' she demanded.

For a moment he was tempted to explain and then a feeling of annoyance took control and he said, 'What the hell has it got to do with you? If you must know, she wants me to go and see her.'

'And you'll go running to her,' Maria stormed jealously. 'She's got you just where she wants you. You're like a puppet on a string.'

He turned and walked out into the night before she could say any more. He took one of the two remaining trucks and drove into Barford, seething with anger. What right had she to say what he should, and should not, do? He cursed and swung the wheel savagely as he skidded on a dangerous bend. She'd appointed herself his conscience, judging everything he did and always finding him guilty. He lit a cigarette and began to calm down. After a while he was even smiling again. Now that he had the money he wouldn't have to put up with her much longer. A few more days at the most.

The truck skidded and lurched over the greasy cobbles of the square and he turned into the side street that led to Jenny O'Connor's flat and pulled into the pavement. He switched off the engine and walked the rest of the way.

He approached the flat cautiously and stood in the entrance of the court, his eyes carefully searching the shadows. After a moment or two he was satisfied and crossed to the door and rang the bell.

There was a short silence before footsteps approached and he heard her call, 'Who is it?'

'It's Marlowe,' he told her.

A bolt was withdrawn and a key clicked in the lock before the door opened to disclose her pale, frightened face. 'What's all the fuss about?' he demanded.

She pulled him inside and locked and bolted the door again before turning to him. 'Oh, Hugh, darling. You've no idea how glad I am to see you.' She threw her arms around his neck.

Marlowe held her for a little while and then gently pushed her away and frowned. 'What's been going on here?'

She led him into the lounge and pulled him down on to the settee beside her. 'I got back late this afternoon,' she said. 'I hadn't been in long when my uncle arrived.' She shuddered at the memory. 'He was almost insane with rage. He said I was a traitor and accused me of helping you. I told him I was leaving.'

'And what was his reaction to that?'

An expression of disgust crossed her face. 'He slapped me twice and knocked me down.' She pulled away the neck of her dress to disclose a livid bruise on her right shoulder. 'Look, that's what he did to me. He said I didn't have the guts to leave him. He took all my money and

110

jewellery. Even my fur coat. He said I'd soon come to my senses.'

Marlowe leaned back, eyes narrowed. 'Frankly, it doesn't sound like a very healthy relationship to me. Did he ever make a pass at you?'

She shook her head. 'No, never. To tell you the truth, I used to wonder at first if he thought about me in that way, but until today he's always behaved perfectly.'

'Why did you lock the door?' Marlowe asked.

She smiled wanly. 'He sent Monaghan round to pick up my car. He tried to get into the house, and I had to slam the door in his face.' An expression of loathing appeared in her eyes. 'He called to me for ages through the letter-box.' She shuddered. 'The things he was saying were horrible.'

Marlowe scowled and clenched a fist. 'Don't worry about that, angel. Next time he crosses my path I intend to pay him back for a few things.'

She went to the cocktail cabinet and poured a whisky and soda. She smiled wryly as she handed it to him. 'What on earth am I going to do, Hugh? I've made such a mess of things.'

Marlowe put his drink down carefully. 'Why did you come back?'

'Because I'm weak,' she said candidly. 'Because the moment I was alone in London this morning, all my good intentions left me and I was afraid. Afraid of being on my own against the world. Afraid of not having any money.'

'Afraid of having to work for a living?' he asked, gently.

She made a face. 'Don't be cruel, Hugh. I know I'm weak. At least I'm honest about it. I came back because I thought I might be able to compromise, but instead I find that I've got to take sides.'

'And whose side are you on?'

An expression of hurt shadowed her eyes. 'Do I have to tell you?' she said. 'Do I really have to tell you?'

He stared into her beautiful, childlike face, and the old warmth moved inside him. He leaned towards her, and she slipped a hand behind his neck and fell backwards against the cushions, pulling him down. He felt the softness of her pressed against him, yielding to him, and he crushed his mouth against hers.

After a while, she pulled away slightly. 'I'm so glad I got through to you before you started for London.'

Marlowe kissed the warm hollow of her neck. 'I'm not going to London.'

'But why not?' she said in surprise. 'I thought it was essential for you to do another trip?'

'It is,' he told her. 'But Mac's gone tonight.'

'Oh, I see.' There was silence for a while and then she said, 'Hugh, what are we going to do?'

He grunted and kissed her shoulder. 'Hell, I don't know,' he said. 'I'll be moving on soon, I suppose.'

She stiffened and said sharply, 'I see.' There was another short silence. 'I believe my uncle called on you this afternoon?'

Marlowe pushed himself up and reached for a cigarette. 'That's right. He had a heart attack, as a matter of fact. I thought at first he was going to peg out on us.'

She played nervously with the collar of her dress. 'Yes, he's had several attacks.' She took a deep breath and went on, 'As a matter of fact I happen to know he's only got six months to live at the most.'

Marlowe paused, his glass half-way to his lips. 'That's interesting,' he said. 'It gives the Magellans some hope, anyway.'

She jumped up angrily. 'Oh, damn the Magellans. Can't you think of anything else?' She paced nervously across the floor and then swung round to face him. 'I'll put it in a nutshell for you. My uncle is going to die. Perhaps tonight or tomorrow, certainly within the next few months, and I'm his sole heir.'

Marlowe swallowed his whisky. 'So what?'

'Can't you see?' she said. 'If only you can persuade the Magellans to sell and we get everything back on an even keel, then it's only a matter of waiting.'

'Waiting for what?' Marlowe said softly.

She sighed impatiently. 'For my uncle to die. Then I'll get the business and you can run it for me. Don't you see, darling? We'll be secure for life.'

Marlowe carefully stubbed out his cigarette and stood up. 'You'll be secure for life, you mean.' He walked past her and went out into the hall.

She ran after him and grabbed at his shoulder as he started to unlock the front door. 'What's wrong?' she demanded. 'What are you doing?'

He pulled away from her and opened the door. 'I'm going,' he said. 'Why shouldn't I? You haven't any claim on me.'

There was an expression of complete shock on her face. She shook her head dumbly. 'I don't understand.'

'I could say it in four-letter words,' Marlow told her, 'but even I have certain standards.' She still looked puzzled, and he sighed. 'Let's put it this way, angel. I've met all sorts, but you take the prize.' He shook his head. 'You don't even know what I'm talking about, do you? People like you never do.'

For a brief moment she continued to stare at him in that dumb, uncomprehending way, and then fury blazed in her eyes and she slashed her hand across his face. 'Get out!' she screamed. 'Go on! Get out!'

He gripped her wrists tightly and held her against him, fury moving inside him. She glared at him for a moment, and spat in his face. And then she called him a certain name.

He stared at her in amazement, and as he released her, he started to laugh. He was still laughing as he crossed the courtyard and went through the dark entry into the street.

He drove back to Litton with the window down, and somehow the cold wind seemed to have a cleansing effect. When he thought of Jenny O'Connor it was with pity. After all, she had to live with herself. That was probably the greatest punishment of all. He deliberately pushed all thoughts of her from his mind and concentrated on examining his own future.

His original idea about going to Ireland still seemed a good one. As he drove into the farmyard he decided to set things in motion at once.

He parked the truck at the front door and went inside. As he walked along the corridor he heard the sound of weeping from the sitting-room. When he looked in, Maria was huddled in a chair sobbing her heart out.

'What is it, angel?' he said, dropping to one knee beside her.

She raised her tear-stained face and said bitterly, 'Get away from me. I can still smell her perfume on you.'

He jumped up in anger. 'For God's sake tell me what all this is about?'

'It's Papa,' she said. 'He's gone out in the other truck.'

Marlowe frowned. 'He must be mad. He's a sick man.'

'I know,' she said. 'Mac phoned through over an hour ago. He'd had a breakdown and asked if you could drive the other truck through to him.'

Marlowe cursed savagely. 'And the old man insisted on going?'

She nodded. 'Yes, while you were having fun with Jenny O'Connor he had to drag himself out of bed and go out on a night like this.'

Before Marlowe could reply, the telephone rang. She rose quickly and answered it. 'Yes, who is it?' she said. There was a short silence as she listened, and then she swayed and clutched at the table. 'What did you say?' She started to shake her head dumbly from side to side, and then she dropped the receiver and turned her agonized face to Marlowe. 'Hugh!' she said. 'Hugh!' She slipped to the floor in a dead faint.

Marlowe dropped to one knee and picked up the receiver. 'Hallo?' he said. 'Marlowe speaking. Who is that?'

'Hugh, is that you?' Mac's voice crackled over the line. 'I'm at a place called Bardon Bank about forty miles away. You'd better get here fast. The old man's dead.'

10

Marlowe arrived at Bardon Bank shortly after seven o'clock on the following morning. It wasn't difficult to locate the scene of the accident. Half-way down the hill a police car and a couple of breakdown wagons were parked at the roadside. He pulled in behind them and switched off the engine.

As he climbed down from the cab, a young police constable approached him with a frown. 'Now then, chum, we don't want any sightseers.'

'The man who crashed was my boss,' Marlowe told him. 'I got a phone call last night telling me to get here as soon as possible.'

An expression of sympathy appeared on the policeman's face. 'Oh yes, your other driver's been here. A Jamaican called Mackenzie. You'll find him at the transport café down at the bottom of the hill.'

Marlowe nodded. 'Thanks. I'd like to have a look before I go, if you don't mind.'

The policeman shrugged. 'Please yourself, but I'm warning you – it isn't very pretty.'

They walked a little way down the road and came to a gaping hole in the wall. The bank fell steeply on the other side through a plantation of firs to a stream fifty or sixty feet below.

The path of the truck was quite plain, and at the end of the lane it had cleared through the fir trees, Marlowe could see the blackened and twisted wreckage of the truck.

He cleared his throat. 'It looks pretty bad.'

The policeman nodded. 'I've been down there, and believe me it *is* bad. The whole damned thing went up in flames when it hit the bottom.'

'What about the old man?' Marlowe said slowly.

The policeman shook his head. 'He's still in there, or what's left of him. They're burning their way through the wreckage now to get him out.'

For a moment longer Marlowe looked down at the wreck,

and then he turned away. 'Thanks,' he said. 'I'll probably see you later.' He climbed back into the truck and drove down to the transport café.

He found Mac sprawled half across a table in one corner, fast asleep. When Marlowe touched him the Jamaican came awake instantly. A slight smile came to his face. 'Hugh! I'd just about given you up.'

Marlowe explained. 'Maria passed out on me when she heard the news. I had to get the doctor in. He gave her a sedative and put her to bed. She was in such a state that I couldn't leave her.'

'How is she now?' Mac asked.

Marlowe shook his head. 'All frozen up inside, poor kid. She's taking it pretty hard. She had a lousy night until I made a cup of tea and slipped a couple of the pills in without telling her. She went out like a light.'

The Jamaican went to the counter and got two cups of coffee. When he returned he said, 'Man, this is a bad business. Mr Magellan shouldn't have turned out on a night like that.'

Marlowe nodded. 'That's what Maria thinks. She blames me. Jenny O'Connor phoned and said she wanted to see me urgently. Maria wasn't too pleased when I went. She thinks I should have been at the farm to take your phone call and come out with the spare truck.'

Mac shook his head. 'But that isn't fair, Hugh. You couldn't have known that I was going to have a break-down.'

Marlowe smiled bitterly. 'Don't give me that crud, Mac. Under the circumstances I should have hung around the farm last night, just in case anything went wrong. I didn't and the old man's dead. Whichever way we look at it, I'm at least partially responsible.'

He pushed a cigarette into his mouth. 'I wonder what caused the accident?'

Mac was tracing patterns on the table with one finger in a pool of spilled tea. 'I was wondering,' he began hesitatingly. 'You don't suppose anything was wrong with the truck, do you?'

Marlowe looked at him inquiringly. 'O'Connor? I don't think so. When was that truck checked last?'

'Yesterday morning,' Mac said. 'I did it myself. It was in good order.'

'That's it then,' Marlowe said. 'There was someone around the place all the time. I can't see how anyone could have tampered with it.'

'What do you think happened?' Mac asked.

Marlowe stared into space and sighed deeply. 'I think Papa Magellan was just a sick, tired, old man who should have been in his bed. He probably passed out at the wheel or perhaps he fell asleep. Whatever happened, it only took a minute.' He stood up. 'Yes, he was just a sick old man who depended on me, and when he needed me most I wasn't around.' He turned and walked rapidly out of the café as the impotent fury surged into his throat in a strangled sob.

It was almost noon when they managed to get what was left of the old man out of the truck. They brought him up the hill wrapped in a blanket, and Marlowe and the Jamaican stood and watched silently as the body was put into the ambulance. As the man in charge of the breakdown team scrambled up, Marlowe walked across to him and said, 'Did you find anything that indicated why he'd run off the road?'

The man shook his head. 'We aren't likely to, either. Not in that heap of scrap.'

Marlowe turned away, sick at heart, and motioned to Mac. 'Come on, let's get out of here,' he said. 'It stinks like a charnel house.'

But all the way back to Litton he was unable to get the stench of burnt flesh out of his nostrils. It stayed with him even when he opened the side windows and filled the cab with air. He told himself it was all in the mind, and took even greater risks, driving into the curves at a dangerous speed, his hands gripping the wheel until his knuckles showed white.

Mac sat quietly beside him, saying nothing. When they finally turned into the farmyard and halted outside the door, he said to Marlowe, 'What you need is a

117

good stiff drink, man. Come on in and I'll get you one.'

Marlowe shook his head. 'No, not for me.'

'What about Maria?' the Jamaican asked. 'She'll need you at a time like this.'

'Need me?' Marlowe said. 'Why should she need me?'

Mac shook his head. 'Man, you must be blind. That girl loves you.'

Marlowe laughed savagely. '*Did* love me, you mean. I'm the man who was responsible for her father's death, remember.' He turned abruptly and walked away across the yard to the barn.

He paused in the entrance to light a cigarette. It tasted like straw and he tossed it away with a curse. He walked forward into the barn, hands in pockets, head bowed down, and then he stiffened as his eyes lighted on something.

He dropped on one knee beside the pool of liquid and dipped a finger into it. He lifted the finger to his nostrils and sniffed deeply, and then he gently touched it to his lips. It was fluid from the hydraulic-braking system of the truck.

For a moment he stayed poised on one knee, paralysed and unable to fully comprehend the meaning of his discovery, and then he got to his feet, murder in his heart, and turned and walked out of the barn towards the truck.

It was all plain now. All very plain. The old man hadn't passed out at the wheel. He'd crashed through that wall because the truck had got out of control on the hill. It had got out of control because somebody had tampered with the brakes. It was as simple as that.

He scrambled behind the wheel of the truck and pulled the starter. The engine roared, drowning Mac's cry in the background, and Marlowe took the truck across the farmyard in a burst of speed and skidded out of the gate into the main road.

As he drove towards Barford he was conscious of one thing only. He was going to kill O'Connor. He was going to wrap his hands round that fat neck and squeeze all life out of the grotesque body. Anyone who got in his way would get stamped into the ground.

It started to rain and lightning forked across the sky. As he turned the truck into the square a clap of thunder tore the heavens apart and rain started to fall in a torrential sheet.

Marlowe braked to a halt in front of O'Connor's place and stepped from the cab on to the loading-platform. The rain buffeted him as he went towards the great sliding-doors. He pulled on them with all his strength, but they refused to yield. There was a small postern gate set slightly to one side, with a Yale lock. He tried the handle several times with no success. He pushed the rain away from his eyes and stood back a little. He took three quick paces forward and stamped his right foot hard against the little door. It burst open with a splintering crash as the lock yielded, and he stepped inside.

An eerie silence reigned except for the hard drumming of the rain against the windows. The warehouse was in half darkness, and he moved forward, senses alert for any sound. There was a slight click and the vast room was flooded with light. 'Who's there?' a voice called.

Marlowe raised his eyes. Blacky Monaghan was standing on the landing at the top of a long flight of wooden stairs. He had been sleeping, and he rubbed his eyes several times and blinked. After a while he seemed to get Marlowe into focus. 'What the hell do you want?' he shouted.

Marlowe approached the bottom of the stairs. 'I want O'Connor,' he said. 'I want O'Connor, and if you try to stop me getting to him I'll kill you.'

Something like fear flickered in the Irishman's eyes. 'You're wasting your time,' he said. 'He isn't here.'

Marlowe started to mount the stairs slowly, his eyes fastened unwinkingly on Monaghan. The Irishman licked his lips and stood back a little. 'I don't want any trouble with you, Marlowe,' he said. 'I've no quarrel with you.'

Marlowe smiled terribly. 'But I've got a quarrel with you, you bastard,' he said.

Stark terror showed in Monaghan's eyes, and his voice cracked like an old woman's. 'I tell you he isn't here,' he said. 'He's at the girl's place. It's the truth, I tell you.' He backed away along the landing as Marlowe neared the top

119

of the stairs and screamed, 'Go on, get out of it. I've told you what you want to know.'

Marlowe shook his head and laughed tightly. 'I haven't finished with you yet,' he said. 'Not by a long way.'

An expression of utter desperation appeared on Monaghan's drink-sodden face. He looked around wildly. Hanging on the wall there was a fire extinguisher, a shovel, and a felling axe, all brightly painted in red. He grabbed at the axe and wrenched it from its fastenings on the wall. He turned to face Marlowe, gibbering with fear, the axe poised. 'Keep away from me,' he shrieked. 'I didn't kill the old man. It was the boss this time. You were supposed to go out in that truck.'

Marlowe stood rooted to the spot, staring at the Irishman, and then a terrible surging fury rushed through him and he sprang forward.

Monaghan swung desperately with the axe. If he'd taken his time and judged the distance he could have split Marlowe's skull on the spot, but blind panic took possession of him. Marlowe ducked and the axe whistled over his head and rang against the wall. One terrible, rending hand gripped Monaghan by the throat and the other relentlessly twisted the axe from his grasp.

Monaghan's face turned purple. With a strength born of panic he kicked forward desperately and caught Marlowe on his right shin. Marlowe grunted in pain and his grip slackened. The Irishman staggered back against the wood railing. As Marlowe came forward he struck out at him desperately. Marlowe took the punch on one shoulder, slammed his left into Monaghan's belly and lifted his knee as the Irishman started to bend.

As the terrible blow in the face sent him backwards, Monaghan bounced against the wooden rail. There was a splintering crash as it gave way and he disappeared below with a single cry.

Marlowe moved forward to the edge of the landing and looked down. He gave a sudden roar of rage. Monaghan had fallen no more than ten or twelve feet on to a great mound of potato sacks. As Marlowe watched, the Irishman rolled to the bottom, lurched to his feet and staggered towards the splintered door through which Marlowe had entered the building. He paused once at the door to glance fearfully over his shoulder, and then he disappeared.

Marlowe jumped down on to the pile of potato sacks, lost his balance, and tumbled to the bottom. He picked himself up and ran across the floor to the door. As he emerged from the warehouse, an engine coughed into life and a small yellow van moved across the square and vanished up a side street.

He pulled himself up behind the wheel and turned the truck towards the street that led to Jenny O'Connor's flat. He was praying that Monaghan had not been lying and that he would find O'Connor there. The quality of the fury which possessed him was such that he was conscious of only one burning thought. He was going to kill O'Connor.

Now he had the definite, final proof from Monaghan's own lips. O'Connor had planned his death, but the plan had misfired and Papa Magellan had died instead. It was fitting that O'Connor should make full and final reparation.

He parked the truck and ran through the rain into the little court. He leaned against the bell, pressing with all his force without stopping, so that the sound of it filled the entire house.

The door opened and Jenny stood before him. He brushed her aside and moved towards the lounge. As he came into the room, O'Connor rose from a seat by the fire, alarm on his face.

Jenny came hurriedly into the room behind him. 'For God's sake, what is it, Hugh?' she demanded. 'What's happened?'

Marlowe kept his eyes fixed on O'Connor. 'Papa Magellan's dead,' he said.

A curious expression appeared on O'Connor's face, and he took out a handkerchief and held it to his lips. Jenny gave a shocked gasp. 'Oh, no, Hugh! Not that poor old man. How did it happen?'

Marlowe nodded towards O'Connor. 'Ask him,' he said. 'He'll tell you. He knows all about it.'

'I don't know what you're talking about,' O'Connor said.

'You bloody swine,' Marlowe said deliberately. 'I've just dealt with Monaghan and he told me what happened. You got him to fix the brakes of one of the trucks. You expected me to go out in it, but unfortunately the old man took the truck out instead.' He laughed savagely. 'Would you be interested to know how he died? I'll tell you. He went through a wall, sixty feet down into a ravine. Then he fried. Have you ever smelt burning human flesh, O'Connor? I have. It's something you never forget.'

O'Connor seemed to be choking into his handkerchief. He took it away from his lips and gasped, 'I didn't have anything to do with it.'

Marlowe started to move towards him. 'I'm going to kill you, O'Connor,' he said. 'I'm going to kill you with my bare hands.'

The fat man dipped his left hand into his pocket. When it came out he was holding an automatic pistol. 'Keep away from me,' he said. He seemed to choke and his face was beginning to turn purple. 'You're going to listen to me, you damned fool.'

As Marlowe paused, O'Connor gurgled horribly and fell backwards into his chair, the pistol slipping from his nerveless hands. Marlowe moved forward and grabbed him by the shirt front. 'You bastard,' he said. 'You needn't think you can trick me this way.'

O'Connor's lips were blue and a line of foam appeared on his mouth. His eyes rolled and he managed to focus them on Marlowe with difficulty. A half-smile appeared on his face and he said faintly, 'You damned fool. You've got to . . .' His eyes swivelled upwards and his head fell limply to one side.

Jenny O'Connor pushed past him as Marlowe stood up, and dropped on her knees beside her uncle. She placed her ear to his chest and listened for several seconds. When she got up there was an expression that was almost triumph on her face. 'He's dead,' she said. 'I knew that heart of his wouldn't last much longer.'

All at once Marlowe felt completely deflated. He stumbled to the cocktail cabinet and splashed brandy into a glass. He poured it down his throat in one clean gulp, and coughed as the liquor burned its way into his stomach.

There was a mirror hanging on the wall and he looked at his reflection and felt apart from it as if it was someone he did not know – had never known. A hand slipped over his shoulder and a warm body was pressed against him. 'This is it, darling,' Jenny said. 'This is what I was talking about. You and me together. We could have everything we wanted.'

He turned, brushing her away as one might a fly, and looked at O'Connor lolling horribly in the chair. 'My God,' he croaked, 'you don't even bother to bury your dead, do you?'

She stared at him, frozen-faced, and he turned and lurched through the door, leaving her there with her dead uncle in her lovely room, surrounded by beautiful things.

It was an appalling drive back to Litton. The rain was falling so heavily that visibility was reduced to ten or fifteen yards and the windscreen-wipers were almost useless.

The cobbles in the farmyard were flooded with rain, and when he jumped down from the truck the water mounted over his shoes, chilling him to the bone. He stood in the hall and peeled off his wet jacket, and then he was conscious of the utter quiet. He stood quite still, his face lifted a little, nostrils moving slightly like some animal that scents danger.

'Mac!' he called. 'Where are you?' His voice echoed hollowly in the uncanny silence.

He mounted the stairs, two at a time, and turned along the landing. 'Mac!' he shouted, and threw open the door of their bedroom. He paused in the doorway, his jacket slipping from his fingers and gazed around him in bewilderment.

The room was a complete shambles. The bedding was scattered in every direction and the mattress had been slashed open exposing the horse-hair stuffing. Every drawer was pulled out and his personal belongings had been emptied on to the floor.

He turned quickly and went downstairs. The kitchen looked as it usually did, except that the fire was out in the old-fashioned grate. He stood in the doorway and his eyes moved slowly over everything.

A shudder ran through him and he moved forward and dropped on one knee beside the table. There was a pool of blood on the floor.

At that moment the telephone rang sharply, its harsh clamour shattering the silence. He ran along the corridor, fear gripping him by the vitals, and lurched into the sitting-room. He snatched up the receiver. 'Hallo, Marlowe here. Who is that?'

The line crackled a little and a voice that was vaguely familiar said, 'Hallo, Hugh, old man. So glad you've got back. This is the fifth time I've phoned during the past hour.'

Marlowe swallowed hard and tried to keep his voice steady. 'Who is that?' he said.

A gay laugh drifted along the line. 'Don't you recognize me, old man? Now really, I'm quite hurt. This is Faulkner speaking.'

Marlowe closed his eyes for a moment and his hand tightened convulsively over the phone. 'How the hell did you find me?'

'Never mind that, old man,' Faulkner told him. 'The point is, we've already visited your present residence and found you out. However, we did find a young lady and a coloured gentleman, and suggested they might like to keep us company for an hour or two.'

Marlowe moistened his lips. 'Get to the point, Faulkner. What do you want?'

'Oh, come now, old man. Don't let's be naïve.'

'I found some blood on the kitchen floor,' Marlowe said. 'Who got hurt. It wasn't the girl, was it?'

Faulkner made an expression of distaste. 'No, it was your Jamaican pal. I'm afraid he didn't quite see eye to eye with us. Butcher had to persuade him a little. But don't worry. He's doing nicely.'

'And the girl?' Marlowe said.

'Oh, she's all right,' Faulkner assured him. 'At the moment, anyway. I'm given to understand you have quite an interest there, old man.'

'Who told you that?' Marlowe croaked.

'Never mind for the moment,' Faulkner said. 'For the young lady's sake I sincerely hope it's true. You'll find us at a place called Garvald Mill about four miles out of Litton. It's just off the Birmingham road. If you're not here within an hour with the twenty thousand, I'll turn the girl over to Harris. You know what he's like where young women are concerned.'

'Faulkner, wait a minute. Listen to me,' Marlowe shouted.

He was wasting his time. There was a slight click and the line went dead.

11

For several moments Marlowe stood holding the receiver to his ear and then he slowly replaced it in its cradle. He went out of the front door and ran across the farmyard, splashing through the heavy rain and not caring.

The ladder was still in position against the loft. For a moment he looked up at it and then he started to climb. The Gladstone bag was exactly where he had left it, and he pulled it from under the old cricket net and climbed quickly down to the ground.

He walked back to the house through the rain, the bag swinging in his right hand, and tried to work out his next move. When he went into the sitting-room he emptied the bag on the table and sat down in a chair and lit a cigarette.

The bundles of notes almost covered the table-top, and one or two had fallen down on to the floor. He stared at them, his heart thudding, and after a while an ironic laugh escaped from his lips. It was really very funny when you considered it. All the years, the long, hard years in the place with the high walls. The grey morning filtering in through the tiny window on to his face, the hopeless queues of men slopping out, the bad food, the squalor, the vice, the rottenness. All these things he had endured and one thing had kept him going. The knowledge that some day he would be free and with enough money to keep him comfortably for the rest of his life.

A man could live very well in a country like Ireland with twenty thousand pounds behind him. He sighed and laughed again. Yes, it was really rather ironic that in the end he should sacrifice all that for a young girl he'd known for a few days only.

He stood up and began to put the money back into the bag. He had tried to pretend to himself for a while that he had a choice, but deep inside he had known that there was only one choice for him. The veneer of toughness, the brutality he had raised like a fence around him during the years against life, could not help him now. He was faced with a simple human problem. It could be solved in one way only. By a sacrifice on his part.

He snapped the bag shut and pushed it on one side. He remembered having seen a map of the district in the sideboard, and he went and got it and spread it out on the table. As he pored over it he felt curiously light-hearted. It was a sensation he found impossible to analyse, even to himself.

Garvald Mill was clearly marked on a side road about a quarter of a mile off the main Birmingham road just outside Litton. He found an old stub of blue pencil in the table drawer, and he drew a circle around the mill and considered the situation.

It was situated on the bank of a stream and the area was heavily wooded. He frowned and went to the sideboard and poured himself a brandy. If it had been a simple matter of going and handing over the money it would have been all right, but Butcher and Harris were there as well. Faulkner was all right in his own twisted way. He

126

did have some kind of code. Butcher and Harris were a different thing entirely. They were twisted in another way, and Marlowe had an uncomfortable feeling that this time they wouldn't be prepared to let him off so easily. Not Harris, certainly. The little man was a psychopath, and once he got started there was no knowing what he would do.

Marlowe remembered Faulkner's threat to turn the girl over to Harris, and he shuddered and went back to the map. The mill was near the edge of a wood, and the approach road turned sharply so that it was possible to move quite close without being seen.

He left the room and went into the kitchen. He opened the drawers until he found the one in which Maria kept her kitchen knives. She had a good selection. He finally chose a hollow-ground carver with a nine-inch blade. In another drawer he found a roll of insulating tape and he quickly cut several strips from it. He pulled up his left trouser-leg and carefully fixed the knife to the inside of his left shin with the strips of tape.

As he turned to leave the kitchen he heard the low rumble of thunder in the distance and the rain started to drum against the windows with increasing force. At that moment the doorbell rang sharply.

He stood still and listened. He could hear voices, and through the stained-glass panel at the side of the door a distorted image was visible. He moved forward slowly as the bell rang again, and opened the door. He looked straight into the kindly, spaniel-like face of Alpin, the Barford policeman. Alpin smiled and said, 'Now then, son, I've brought an old friend of yours along to see you. He's very anxious to have a few words with you.'

He stood slightly to one side and Superintendent Masters moved forward. 'Hallo, Marlowe,' he said. 'Fancy seeing you here.'

Marlowe stared at him, completely off guard, and Alpin grinned. 'You don't mind if we come in, do you? It's rather wet out here.'

They brushed past him and entered the hall. As he closed the door, Alpin continued, 'We'll go in here, if it's all right with you. I think we ought to have a few words.' He led the way into the sitting-room and Masters followed.

Marlowe stood in the doorway and watched them carefully. Masters started to light his pipe and, as he did so, leaned over the table and examined the map. 'Hallo, what's all this? Planning to make a trip?' he said. 'Bag packed and everything.'

He reached over and clicked the Gladstone bag open. There was a moment's silence as Alpin moved over and looked into the bag, and then Masters whistled. 'Funny looking stuff, isn't it?' He snapped the bag shut and shook his head. 'And to think what some men are prepared to do for it.'

'Aye, there's no accounting for taste,' Alpin observed, taking out his inhaler and sniffing deeply.

Marlowe made an exclamation of impatience. 'Let's cut out all the clever stuff and get down to essentials,' he said. 'How did you find me?'

It was Alpin who gave him his answer. 'My God, what do you think we do in the police force? Sit around on our backsides all day? The afternoon of the morning you had your first run-in with Monaghan and his two pals behind O'Connor's place, there was a full description of you going out over the wire.'

Masters smiled and puffed at his pipe. 'You see, Marlowe, even country policemen aren't quite as stupid as you tough boys seem to imagine. Do you really think a policeman doesn't give it any thought when a man like you arrives in a small country town and immediately takes on the three worst toughs in the place, single-handed?' He grinned. 'We've got files at Scotland Yard. There aren't many well-spoken young men of six feet four who favour the spade as a weapon. It took a day or two, but finally it reached me.'

Suddenly, Marlowe was filled with rage. He saw everything now. 'You lousy swine,' he snarled. 'You found out where I was and then sicked Faulkner and his mob on to me.'

Masters looked genuinely astonished. 'I don't know what you're talking about,' he said.

Marlowe was almost insane with rage. He took a quick step forward and swung a tremendous punch at the policeman's jaw. In his anger he miscalculated badly and the blow missed Masters by several inches. He grabbed Marlowe by the arm and twisted him round and Alpin moved in quickly and grabbed his other wrist.

'Now use your bloody head,' Masters said forcefully. 'You've known me a long time, Marlowe. When did I ever play a trick like that on anyone?'

Marlowe relaxed completely. It was true. Masters was incapable of that sort of a trick. He had a reputation, even amongst the criminal fraternity, for being utterly fair and honest in his methods.

As they released him Marlowe turned and said, 'I'm sorry. I got things a bit twisted.'

'You've had things twisted for quite a while,' Masters told him. He patted the bag. 'It was all for nothing, Marlowe. If you'd had the sense to tell us where the money was at your trial you'd have got five years at the most. Instead, you were stubborn and the judge took that into account. You've served two extra years in prison and for nothing.'

Marlowe made an impatient movement. 'All right, so I was a mug, but there's something more important to discuss at the moment. You can't take that money now. I need it.' They stared at him in complete surprise and he went on, 'Faulkner's been here. That's why I was so mad. I thought you'd told him where I was. He's taken Maria Magellan with him. I had a telephone message a little while ago. He's given me an hour in which to hand over the money or else.' He glanced at the clock. 'I've only got thirty minutes left.'

Masters laughed coldly. 'Now really, Marlowe, you don't expect us to believe a story like that, do you? Let's face the facts. You were just getting ready to pull out of here.'

A feeling like panic moved in Marlowe. 'You've got to believe me. You can search the house. You won't find the girl here.'

Masters turned to Alpin and raised his eyebrows. 'What do you think?' he asked.

Alpin frowned and then moved over to the window. 'I know Maria Magellan and in the ordinary way of things she would be here.' He sighed. 'Unfortunately her father's just been killed in a road accident. She couldn't very well stay here on her own with Marlowe and Mackenzie.'

Masters nodded. 'That sounds reasonable.' He turned to Marlowe and shook his head. 'Sorry, chum, we aren't buying today.'

Marlowe was calm and completely sure of himself now. He took one step forward and this time he made no mistake. His left fist sank into Masters's stomach and the big policeman doubled over, the breath hissing out of his body.

Marlowe was out of the room and closing the door even as Alpin moved. He slammed the front door behind him and ran out into the rain. He scrambled up behind the wheel of the truck and switched on the engine. He was half-way across the yard and moving into second gear as the door opened and Alpin appeared in the porch.

The rain was slanting into the earth in solid sheets like glass and thunder rolled ominously in the distance. He wiped rain away from his eyes and concentrated on the road ahead. It was almost impossible to see through the windscreen and he couldn't afford accidents at this stage.

He glanced quickly at his watch. He still had twenty minutes in which to reach the mill, though what he was going to do when he got there was anybody's guess. The truck roared up the hill past the railway station, and a slight ironic smile twisted his lips as he passed the spot in the hedge through which he had squeezed on the fateful day he had arrived in Litton. He recalled everything that had happened. Perhaps he should never have got off the train? He shook his head. That was no answer. Life was a game and you never knew how

130

the cards were going to fall from one minute to the next.

He braked, his foot hard against the pedal, and swung the truck into the narrow lane that led to Garvald Mill. He frowned and tried to recall the map in detail. The mill, he had calculated, was a quarter of a mile from the road, and it came into view rather unexpectedly round a bend. He slowed down and pulled the truck into the side of the road and halted.

He jumped down into the rain and went forward on foot. About fifty yards farther along the road was the bend, and when he reached it he cut into the woods and forced his way through a fir plantation towards the mill, dimly seen through the trees.

He crouched down under a bush and examined the place carefully. The bulk of the building consisted of a large, three-storeyed tower, roof gaping to the sky. Built on to the building was an extension in wood which looked rather like stables or a storehouse. It seemed to be in a slightly better state of repair than the rest of the building. At the far side there was an immense water-wheel, and it was moving round now with an unearthly creaking and groaning, forced by the rushing waters of the flooded stream.

Marlowe frowned for a moment as he considered his next move, and then he sighed and got to his feet. There was really nothing he could do except take a chance and hope that something would turn up. He stepped out into the open and walked towards the mill.

When he was a few yards away, the door of the wooden part of the building opened and Faulkner appeared. He smiled cheerfully and called, 'Good show, Hugh. I knew I could depend on you. I always did say you had slightly nobler basic instincts than the rest of us.'

He stood back slightly and Marlowe walked past him into the building. The place smelled of old hay and mice. There was a decrepit cart in one corner and a large loft ran round three sides of the building, with round, glassless windows letting in light.

131

In the centre of the room there was an old five-gallon oil-can with a fire burning in it. As Marlowe moved forward his eyes quickly passed over everything. He could hear the water-wheel splashing violently outside, and against the stone wall of the mill itself there was a pool of water, covered with green scum and surrounded with stones smoothed by the years.

Butcher and Harris were sitting by the fire on wooden boxes, and their eyes fastened on him malignantly, burning with hate. 'Hallo, Marlowe,' Butcher said. 'I didn't think you'd come. I was wrong.'

'When were you ever right, you pig?' Marlowe said.

He turned away as Butcher half rose, and Faulkner quickly said, 'Now then, don't let's have any fuss, boys.'

Marlowe laughed harshly. 'They don't bother me,' he said. 'They don't even interest me. I want to see the girl and the Jamaican. Where are they?'

Faulkner smiled and walked over to the corner which was nearest the pool of water. There was a pile of old hay that smelled as if it had been mouldering there for years. He pulled some of it aside and disclosed the forms of Maria and the Jamaican. They were both bound and gagged.

'Take their gags out,' Marlowe ordered.

For a moment Faulkner hesitated, and then he shrugged. As he pulled away the Jamaican's gag, Mac smiled. 'Hallo, boy. I knew you wouldn't let us down.'

'Are you okay?' Marlowe asked.

Mac grinned. 'That big dumb ox there cracked me on the head a little, but I'll survive.'

Maria gave a broken sob as her mouth was freed. 'Oh, Hugh, thank God you've come. What's this all about? What do these men want?'

Marlowe smiled reassuringly. 'Don't worry, angel. I'll have you out of here in a few minutes.'

He turned and walked back to the fire and Faulkner followed him. 'Well, are you satisfied?' he asked Marlowe.

Marlowe nodded. 'I'll get you the money now.'

The two men by the fire stood up quickly, and Faulkner frowned. 'You mean you haven't got it on you?'

Marlowe held up a hand. 'There's no need to panic,' he said. 'Did you think I was mug enough to walk in here without seeing what the situation was first?' He shrugged. 'I hid the bag containing the money under a bush a little way into the wood. I'll have to go and get it.'

Faulkner smiled. 'I should have known,' he said. 'You always were a little brighter than anyone else.' He motioned to Butcher. 'You go with him and watch him closely.' He took his hand out of his pocket and held up a Luger automatic pistol. 'No funny business, Marlowe. Remember the girl and your pal will still be here with Harris and me.'

Marlowe opened the door without a word and walked across the clearing towards the wood. He plunged in without looking back and Butcher followed him. As they pushed their way forward, Butcher cursed and said, 'You would pick a place like this, Marlowe. I'm soaked to the skin already.'

Marlowe pushed a large branch to one side and started to speak. 'I'm not very interested in how you feel, Butcher.' He let the branch sweep backwards into Butcher's face.

He turned quickly, and as Butcher staggered back with a curse he flung himself forward and hit him across his throat with the edge of the hand. Butcher fell to the ground, choking and moaning faintly. Marlowe drew back his foot and kicked him savagely in the side of the head, and then, without stopping, he started back towards the mill, bearing slightly to the left.

He came out on to the bank of the stream about thirty or forty yards above the mill. The flood waters rushed past him, brown and foam-flecked, bearing all before them. For a brief moment he considered the position, and then he lifted his trouser-leg and pulled the knife from its hiding-place. He held it securely in his right hand and grasping the branches of a small bush that drooped into the stream, slid down the bank and lowered himself into the water.

For a moment he hung there, and then, as the current tugged at his body, he released his grip on the bush and was immediately carried away. At that point the stream was only three or four feet deep and as he was carried towards the mill, his feet scrabbled on the bottom as he tried to keep his balance.

And then the water deepened and he was swimming, kicking strongly with every ounce of strength that he possessed. Quite suddenly he was carried over a concrete apron and fell four or five feet into a deep pool. As he struggled to the surface the great, lumbering mill wheel thundered above his head, churning the water into white foam.

The current carried him relentlessly towards it and a terrible panic moved inside him. He thrashed his legs desperately and then a peculiar twist of the current came to his aid and swept him in behind the wheel against the moss-covered stone foundations of the mill.

For several moments he stayed there, hanging on to a ledge of stone with his left hand and coughing up the brown river water. He found, to his surprise, that he still held the knife in his right hand and he renewed his grip on it with white, numbed fingers. The water was icy and now that he was not moving he was conscious of the coldness of it seeping into him, chilling him to the bone.

He placed the knife carefully between his teeth, took a deep breath and sank down under the surface of the stream, his hands scrabbling at the rough stones of the foundations, pulling himself downwards. The great wheel revolved through the water alarmingly near to his body and panic moved again in him as an unexpected current pulled at his legs and one foot touched the wheel as it went round.

He surfaced once for air and then dived again. There had to be an outlet to that pool inside the mill and he dragged himself along the stones, his eyes straining through the brown, cloudy water. And then he found what he was looking for. It was the entrance to a low, arched tunnel some three feet high and half-way down the wall.

He decided to take a chance and pulled himself into it without surfacing for air. To his surprise he discovered that no more than the thickness of the mill wall separated the pool from the stream itself. He kicked forward and carefully surfaced through the green scum.

He kept well in to the side and raised only his eyes and nose above the surface of the water. Harris and Faulkner were standing over by the half-open door, peering outside.

'I don't like it,' Harris was saying. 'I never did trust Marlowe. He was always a tricky bastard.'

'For God's sake shut up,' Faulkner said impatiently. 'They've only been gone a short time.'

Very carefully Marlowe pulled himself over the edge of the pool and crawled towards the corner where Maria and the Jamaican were lying. As he approached, Mac turned his head and his face lit up. At the same moment Maria noticed him and she opened her mouth in an involuntary gasp.

Marlowe burrowed into the hay and froze for several moments, but the two men at the door didn't notice and after a while he moved beside the Jamaican and quickly sliced through his bonds. 'Whatever happens don't make a sound,' he mouthed.

As he crawled to Maria and started to free her, Mac said in a low voice, 'What do we do now?'

Marlowe didn't get a chance to reply. At that moment Harris turned and idly glanced across to the corner. His mouth dropped and for a moment he was speechless. He found his voice and grabbed at Faulkner's arm. 'He's in here,' he screamed. 'The bastard's tricked us.'

Faulkner swung round, the Luger in his right hand, and Marlowe turned and ran crouching for the pool. As the first shot thundered at him he flung himself head first into the pool and dived for the outlet. His hands clawed fiercely at the stones and then he was outside and surfacing.

There wasn't a moment to be lost and he released his grip on the wall and let himself drift out from under the wheel. The current swung in towards the bank, carrying him before it, and he clutched fiercely at a trailing branch from a tree and pulled himself out of the water.

Beside him a stone outbuilding leaned against the great bulk of the mill, and a few feet above it the lower windows gaped like sightless eyes. He jumped for the flat roof of the outbuilding, his fingers gripping the edge securely, and pulled himself up.

The sill of the first window was only three feet above the roof of the outbuilding and its glass was long since shattered. In a moment he was standing inside. He found himself in an empty, decaying room and he crossed quickly to a door and opened it. Outside there was a narrow corridor and another door hung crazily on one hinge in front of him. He could hear voices quite clearly and he tiptoed cautiously across the room towards the round window. He found himself looking down into the loft of the building he had just left so hurriedly.

Faulkner was standing near the fire, the Luger pointed threateningly at Maria and the Jamaican. Harris was cursing at the top of his voice. 'He's tricked us,' he raved. 'He'd no intention of bringing the money.'

'Shut your trap,' Faulkner said. 'And let me think this out.'

Harris turned and his eyes lighted on Maria. He pulled his flick-knife from his pocket and started towards her. 'I'll make the bastard sorry,' he said viciously. 'He won't recognize his girl-friend when I've finished with her.'

Mac jumped up and stood in front of Maria. 'You lay a finger on her and I'll kick your face in if it's the last thing I do on earth.'

Faulkner turned the gun menacingly towards Harris and said, 'Don't be stupid, you little fool. That won't get us anywhere now.'

Marlowe clambered through the round window and lowered himself gently on to the loft. The boards creaked a little and he crouched down and worked his way over to the edge on his hands and knees.

Harris and Faulkner were arguing furiously and then, as Marlowe looked desperately about him for a possible weapon, there was the sound of vehicles drawing up outside.

Faulkner ran quickly to the door and looked out. After a moment he turned, his face pale, and said tightly, 'It's the police. Superintendent Masters of all people.'

Masters's voice was raised outside. 'Marlowe, are you in there?'

Mac shouted at the top of his voice. 'Watch yourselves. There's a guy with a gun in here.'

There was a short silence and then Alpin's voice was heard. 'If you've got any sense you'll throw that gun down and come out.'

Faulkner started to laugh. He took out an elegant case and selected a cigarette and then lit it with a gold lighter. 'It's rather funny, really,' he said.

Harris cursed. 'You're off your rocker. We've got to get out of here.'

Faulkner shook his head gently. 'That's the trouble with your kind, Harris. You never know when it pays to give up. I do.'

Harris stared at him in amazement and said furiously, 'What do you mean, give up? There's no need. We've got the gun and the girl as a hostage. We can walk out of here with no trouble.'

Faulkner shook his head pityingly. 'It doesn't even work when they do it in the films,' he said.

He turned and started to walk towards the door. Harris took a hurried step after him, the blade clicked open in his knife and he plunged it into Faulkner's back.

As Faulkner crumpled to the floor several things happened at once. Maria screamed loud and long and the door began to shake as the police started to break it down.

Harris snatched up the Luger, which had fallen from Faulkner's hand, and loosed a shot at the door. There was a line of white foam on his lips and he giggled horribly and fired two more shots through the door.

The banging ceased abruptly and Harris drew a hand across his eyes and turned. His eyes fastened on Maria and the Jamaican and a terrible expression appeared on his face. As he started to raise the weapon, Marlowe shouted, 'I'm here, Harris!' And vaulted to the floor.

The shock jarred his whole body and he bent at the knees and rolled over in a somersault. Harris turned and fired

137

wildly. 'I've got you, you bastard,' he shrieked. 'I've got you.'

As he fired again, Marlowe rolled over desperately and reached for the oil drum containing the fire. A bullet scoured a furrow along one shoulder and then his hands fastened on the oil drum and he turned, lifted it aloft and dashed it straight into the madman's face.

Harris gave a ghastly scream and staggered back, the gun falling from his hand. He got to his feet and ran towards the door, his clothes ablaze, beating at the flames with his bare hands. He pulled the locking bar from its socket, wrenched open the door and disappeared outside into the rain, still screaming.

Maria ran forward and threw herself into Marlowe's arms. 'Oh, thank God, Hugh. Thank God,' she cried and broke into passionate sobs.

Marlowe winced as he gently touched her with his hands. Great blisters were beginning to show on his palms and some of the skin was blackened and raw. He handed the weeping girl over to Mac and turned to Faulkner.

Faulkner's breathing sounded bad and as Marlowe dropped on one knee beside him, a trickle of blood oozed from one corner of his mouth. He grinned faintly and said, 'You clever bastard, Marlowe. I always did say you were a little brighter than the rest of us.'

Faulkner closed his eyes, a spasm of pain moving through his body and Marlowe shook him gently. 'Faulkner, who told you I was hiding out in Litton? Was it Masters?'

Faulkner opened his eyes and a ghost of a smile appeared on his lips. 'Good God, no,' he said. 'It was an acquaintance of yours. A white-haired girl called O'Connor. I was having breakfast in a restaurant in Shaftesbury Avenue the other morning when she came up to me as bold as brass and asked me if I knew you.'

Marlowe was conscious of movement beside him and he looked up into Masters's face. He shook his head. 'He's had it,' he said.

As he turned back Faulkner shook his head several times and smiled faintly. 'Poor Hugh. I told you never to trust

138

women, but you always were tender-hearted underneath that surface toughness.' He started to laugh. 'It's damned funny, really.' He choked suddenly and blood rushed from his mouth in a bright stream as his head lolled to one side.

Marlowe got to his feet slowly, his mind seething with conflicting emotions. He felt a hand on his shoulder and turned to gaze into Mac's troubled eyes. 'He was lying, Hugh,' Mac said. 'He must have been. Miss Jenny wouldn't do a thing like that.'

Marlowe shook his head. 'He wasn't lying, Mac. A man doesn't lie when he's dying. Nobody's that sure of where he's going.'

He slipped a hand round Maria's shoulders and helped her towards the door and Masters walked beside them. 'I'm sorry about this, Marlowe,' he said. 'It's a case of cry wolf, I suppose. We just didn't believe you until you took off without the money. Then Alpin looked at the map and found the circle you'd drawn around Garvald Mill. He called in a few reinforcements and we thought we'd take a look.'

'What about Harris?' Marlowe said.

Marlowe shrugged. 'He's in a bad way. They've taken him away in a car.' He shook his head. 'Those burns looked pretty bad.'

Marlowe shrugged. 'I'm not sorry. He stabbed Faulkner in the back and he was going to finish off Mackenzie and the girl. I had to do something pretty drastic.'

Masters sighed. 'Yes, I suppose you did. You always do seem to end up doing something drastic to somebody, don't you?'

They reached the two police cars that were parked on the edge of the clearing and Alpin came up, a lugubrious expression on his face. 'Well, you've given us a little action for once.' His eyes fastened on Marlowe's wounded shoulder and he clicked his tongue. 'We'd better have something done to that. I want you to survive till you've answered all my questions.'

Maria and the Jamaican got into the back of one of the cars and Marlowe stood against the door, the rain beating into him, while a young constable fastened a pad of cotton wool over the groove in his shoulder with surgical tape from a first-aid box.

As the constable dabbed iodine on Marlowe's hands, pain ran through him in great waves, but he was hardly conscious of it. His mind could only concentrate with a terrible burning force on one thing only. That Jenny O'Connor had played him false. That she had tricked him all along the line. That she was responsible for the death of Papa Magellan and he knew, with a terrible sureness, that he was going to kill her.

12

Marlowe stood in the porch and watched the last of the police cars turn out of the gate into the main road. The sound of its engine dwindled into the distance and he lit a cigarette awkwardly, because of his heavily bandaged hands, and stepped out into the driving rain.

As he walked down to the barn, he heard his name called from the house and Mac came out of the porch and ran towards him, splashing through the many pools. Marlowe kept on walking and was entering the barn as the Jamaican caught up with him. Mac pulled at his arm. 'Hey, man, where are you going?'

Marlowe jerked away from him and went over to the work-bench. He pulled open various drawers and searched through them. After a moment or two he grunted with satisfaction and took out a pair of heavy leather driving mitts. 'I can just about get these on.'

Mac frowned. 'What is this, Hugh? You've been acting kind of strange since we got back.'

Marlowe shrugged impatiently. 'I'm all right,' he said. 'Don't worry about me. How's Maria?'

The Jamaican smiled. 'She's in the kitchen making a

meal. Man, she's really come out of all this well. Most girls would have been flat on their backs after what she's been through.' He nodded his head. 'There's a lot of good stuff in that girl.'

Marlowe stared into the middle distance and eased the gloves over his bandaged hands. 'Yes, she's a good kid,' he said. 'She'll make some bloke a fine wife.' He shook his head as if he was dazed and continued, 'Listen, Mac, have you any idea where Monaghan lives?'

Mac nodded. 'Sure, he hangs out in a pub called the Grey Goose. It's in Dover Street not far from the main square.' He frowned. 'What do you want to know for?'

Marlowe bared his teeth and clapped him on the shoulder. 'Nothing important,' he said. 'I just want a word with him.'

He turned to the truck and Mac grabbed him by the arm. 'Is he the only one you're going to have a word with? You sure you're not going after Jenny O'Connor?'

Marlowe swung on him savagely. 'You listen to me,' he said, 'and listen good. Papa Magellan didn't fall asleep at the wheel like we thought. His brakes were fixed. As far as I'm concerned that means he was murdered. O'Connor may have been running things, but she was working with him all along, making a sucker out of me. She must have known what O'Connor intended to do. That makes her just as guilty.'

He pulled himself up behind the wheel and slammed the door. As he started the engine, Mac clambered up on the footboard and said desperately, 'If that's true, it's a police job. You should have told those coppers.' He shook his head. 'You can't go taking any private vengeance, man. They'll hang you just as high as they will her.'

Marlowe pushed him in the chest, sending him staggering back against the wall. 'Sorry, Mac,' he said. 'This is my affair and I'll handle it in my own way. Look after Maria.' He gunned the motor and roared out of the barn before the Jamaican could argue any more.

It was growing dark as he entered the outskirts of Barford and the heavy rain made visibility even poorer. He found Dover Street without difficulty and an illuminated glass sign swinging over the pavement in the rain, indicated the Grey Goose.

As he approached he saw a familiar yellow van parked outside and Monaghan in the act of getting in. The van moved quickly away from the kerb and Marlowe increased speed and followed it.

He wondered where Monaghan was going. Perhaps to meet Jenny O'Connor, but somehow he didn't think so. It was more likely the Irishman was deserting the sinking ship while the going was good.

The van turned into another square and halted in front of the railway station. As Monaghan was getting out of the cab Marlowe parked behind him and jumped down from the cab. 'Going somewhere, Monaghan?' he said.

The Irishman was taking a suitcase out of the cab of the van. He turned and looked at Marlowe in alarm and his jaw dropped. 'What do you want?' he said.

'I want a few more facts from you, Monaghan.' Marlowe spoke softly. 'Mainly about Jenny O'Connor.'

The Irishman threw the suitcase at Marlowe's head and turned and ran for the station steps.

Marlowe ducked and went after him. Monaghan disappeared into the entrance and when Marlowe followed him in, he found that the booking hall was quite crowded. He glanced about him hastily. There was no sign of the Irishman.

He walked over to the ticket barrier and saw, from a notice chalked on a blackboard, that the next train was the London express leaving in five minutes. He quickly bought a platform ticket and passed through the barrier.

The train was standing at a platform on the far side of the track and as he passed over the footbridge, he caught a glimpse of Monaghan getting into a compartment about half-way along the train. He quickly descended the steps leading to the platform and hurried along, peering in through the windows of the compartments. As he reached the end of that particular coach, he saw Monaghan settling in a corner seat.

142

Their eyes met. A look of rage mingled with fear passed over the Irishman's face. He got up quickly and disappeared into the corridor. Marlowe moved to the nearest door, pushed an indignant passenger out of the way and entered the carriage.

As he turned into the corridor, he saw Monaghan disappear round the corner at the far end. Marlowe went after him, pushing his way along the crowded corridor, using his great size ruthlessly to force a passage. People were calling out angrily, somewhere behind him a woman screamed and then he pushed through the last door in the passenger section of the train and found himself in the guard's van.

As he entered, Monaghan was going out of the loading door on to the platform, pushing his way through the porters who were loading the van. Marlowe tripped over a suitcase as he followed and went sprawling on his face, hands outstretched to break his fall. He half-screamed in agony as pain coursed through his tortured hands and then he was on his feet and following Monaghan, who was running like a hare for the far end of the platform.

Slowly Marlowe overhauled him. The Irishman paused at the end of the platform and glanced back and then he turned and jumped down on to the track. There were several goods trains parked a few hundred yards away across a welter of tracks and he made towards them.

As Marlowe followed he heard the sound of an approaching train. He turned his head and saw a fast passenger train entering the station at the other end. Monaghan saw it also and redoubled his efforts to pass across the track, obviously hoping that the train would cut him off from his pursuer. Marlowe gritted his teeth and increased his speed.

There was a dreadful pain in his side and a red mist before his eyes. Somewhere near at hand he could hear the sound of the train. His stride increased and he flung himself forward and fell head first across the rails. The noise of the train was deafening and then, as he scrambled to his feet, he discovered that it was behind him.

Monaghan had disappeared behind the trucks of a near-by goods train. When Marlowe approached, he saw a steep bank on the far side of the train that lifted to a five-foot wire fence and the road beyond. Monaghan was half-way up the bank.

As Marlowe staggered forward the Irishman gave a despairing cry, his foot slipped and he fell backwards, sliding and slipping until he landed in a heap on the track.

Marlowe lifted him up in his great, glove-covered hands and Monaghan babbled in fear, 'For God's sake, Marlowe. Leave me alone. I'll tell you anything you want, only leave me alone.'

Marlowe slapped him back-handed, rocking his head to one side. 'Tell me about Jenny O'Connor and tell me fast. Did she know you were going to tamper with the brakes on my truck?' He shook the Irishman like a rat. 'Tell me!' he said savagely. 'I've got to know.'

Monaghan coughed and tried to pull the hands away from his throat. 'Of course she knew, you fool,' he gasped. 'She was the boss. She arranged everything.'

For a moment Marlowe's hands relaxed as his mind tried to grasp the full meaning of what the Irishman had said and Monaghan fell back against the bank. 'She was pumping you for information all the time,' he went on. 'It was because of what you told her that we knew you were going to truck stuff down to London.'

Marlowe still couldn't believe it. 'But why?' he demanded. 'What about O'Connor?'

Monaghan shrugged and felt his throat tenderly. 'They were married,' he said. 'She was a chorus girl in a cheap strip show. She was appearing in Birmingham when O'Connor saw her. They were married within a week. She made him promise to keep it a secret. He was crazy about her. He would have crawled on his belly from here to London if she'd told him to. He was always small time before. She was the one with all the ideas. She made him start the wholesaling racket and a few other things as well.'

144

Marlowe's mind was numb, but in some curious fashion his brain was as cold as ice. 'What happened the night you fixed the brakes on my truck?'

Monaghan shrugged. 'She thought you'd be going to London that night. She wanted to get you out of the way so that I could have a chance to work on the truck.'

Marlowe reached forward and grabbed the Irishman with his left hand. 'That's all I wanted to know, you dirty swine.' His right fist thudded again and again into Monaghan's face.

Somewhere a police whistle sounded, high and shrill through the rain. Marlowe released his grip on the unconscious body of the Irishman and scrambled hastily up the bank to the fence at the top. As he clambered over it he looked back and saw three policemen running across the tracks towards the goods train.

It was almost completely dark now. He ran along the pavement and turned into the first side street and kept on running. The police could have him afterwards if they wanted, but not now. He had work to do. He had to settle with Jenny O'Connor.

He ran on past the yellow street lamps, through the streets deserted in the heavy rain and after several minutes, came out into the main square. For a moment he hesitated and then he made his decision and turned into the side street that led to her flat.

The little courtyard was quiet and deserted and no light shone from the windows. He leaned against the door and pressed the bell push, but no one answered to its insistent demand.

He turned with a curse and went back the way he had come, back into the rainswept square and started to run towards the warehouse. A great fear had taken possession of him, a fear that she might have left. That he was perhaps too late.

The front of the warehouse was in darkness and when he climbed up on to the loading bay he found the small postern still smashed and hanging crazily on its hinges, as he had left it earlier that afternoon.

He moved through it and stood in the soundless dark. A line of light showed beneath a door in the far corner and he moved quietly towards it and stood for a moment listening. There was no sound. He opened the door and stepped through.

He was in the garage at the rear of the building. Before him, great double doors stood open to the night and a concrete ramp sloped steeply to a loading platform in the basement. As he stood there looking about him, there was the sudden roar of an engine and a truck turned in through the doors and rolled to a halt beside him. Jenny O'Connor looked at him in surprise for a moment or two and then she switched off the engine, applied the handbrake and jumped down from the cab.

She was wearing the black leather driving jacket and tight jeans. Her hair gleamed in the harsh white light of the lamp. She looked altogether lovely and desirable. A peculiar smile appeared on her face. 'Well, Hugh, what is it this time?'

'You lousy rotten bitch,' Marlowe said, in a dead voice.

Something flickered in her eyes. 'So you know?' She laughed harshly. 'Poor Hugh, you were so sure of yourself. So sure of your strength in every way. But I made a fool of you, didn't I?'

He shook his head slowly from side to side. 'All that stuff about your father,' he said. 'All lies. And the tales you told me about O'Connor.' He made an exclamation of disgust. 'And to think you were sleeping with that fat slug.' He shook his head again. 'What kind of a woman are you?'

Anger flared in her eyes. 'I was born in a tenement in Poplar,' she said. 'Maybe that doesn't mean anything to you, but it did to me. Five in a bed, filth and squalor and poverty.' She shook her head. 'That wasn't for me. All my life I've struggled to get on and when I met O'Connor, I seized my chance with both hands. Marrying him meant everything. Comfort, luxury and security.'

'And no price was too high to pay,' Marlowe said. 'Even to killing a poor old man who never harmed you.'

146

She shrugged. 'The old fool got in the way and, anyway, you were supposed to be in that truck.' She laughed in a curious brittle fashion. 'You know I liked you, Hugh Marlowe. I really liked you more than any man I've ever known. I gave you your chance and you wouldn't take it.' Her voice hardened and she said contemptuously: 'The trouble with you is that you're soft underneath. Really soft.' She shook her head. 'You'll never amount to anything.'

Marlowe was having difficulty in contracting his burnt fingers. He wondered in a detached way how he was going to kill her. 'Your little scheme to sick my old pals from London on to me came unstuck,' he said. 'Faulkner's dead and the other two are in the hands of the police.'

A frown appeared on her brow that was quickly erased. 'That's their hard luck,' she said.

Marlowe was beginning to feel a little faint. He passed a hand over his brow. 'Papa Magellan's death was murder. Doesn't that worry you?'

For a moment she was surprised and then an expression of amusement appeared on her face. 'Don't make me laugh,' she said. 'Even if they can prove anything, they can't put a finger on me. My late lamented husband was the boss here as far as anyone knew. He'll take any blame that's going and he's dead.'

She gazed around her at the building and the trucks parked on either side and said with satisfaction, 'Yes, he's dead and all this is mine now.' She smiled at Marlowe pityingly. 'And you could have shared it.' She took a deep breath and said harshly, 'Go on, get out of here, you stupid fool. You're on my property.'

She turned and walked away down the ramp towards the loading bay at the bottom. When she reached it, she took down a vehicle schedule and stood against the loading platform with her back to Marlowe and examined it.

Marlowe looked through the open door into the cab of the truck. In her hurry she had omitted to put the truck

147

into reverse gear and it was held on the steep slope only by the handbrake.

Marlowe looked at the heavy truck, at the steep slope and Jenny O'Connor standing against the platform at the bottom and knew what he must do.

He moved forward and stretched out his hand to the handbrake. There was a gentle cough from behind and a voice said, 'Now that would be a very silly thing to do, son.'

Alpin moved out of the darkness and came forward, shaking rain from his hat, a uniformed sergeant and constable at his shoulder. 'It's you,' Marlowe said stupidly.

Alpin put a hand on his arm and said gently: 'The police handle this sort of thing much better, you know. It's about time you found that out, isn't it?'

Marlowe shook his head. 'But you haven't any proof?'

Alpin smiled and replaced his hat on his head. 'Monaghan's at the station now,' he said. 'He was unconscious when they brought him in, but he recovered enough to give me a few very interesting facts.' He gave Marlowe a gentle shove. 'Go on, get out of here. Your pal's waiting for you outside.'

He turned and went down the ramp towards Jenny O'Connor, the men in uniform walking with him. She turned to face them and as Marlowe watched, Alpin began to speak to her. For a moment she faced him boldly and then her shoulders dropped and she became an old woman.

As Marlowe turned and walked away he remembered the long years, the grey years in the tiny cells, with a little sunlight filtering in through small windows and he wondered how she would look after ten years of that. Would her loveliness last or would it wither away and wrinkle like an apple stored in a dark cupboard for too long?

A truck was standing at the kerbside, its engine gently ticking over and Mac called quietly, 'Over here, Hugh.'

Marlowe climbed up into the passenger seat and the Jamaican drove away. After a while he said, 'I had to tell the police, Hugh. I couldn't stand by and see you ruin yourself. She just isn't worth it.'

Marlowe nodded. 'That's all right, Mac,' he said and then, as an afterthought: 'The other truck's still parked outside the station.'

Mac shrugged. 'We'll pick it up tomorrow.'

Tomorrow, Marlowe thought. So there's going to be a tomorrow, is there? He suddenly realized that he was soaked to the skin and a tremendous wave of tiredness ran through him. 'How's Maria?'

Mac grinned. 'Plenty worried about you, man, but that's all.'

The rain had stopped and Marlowe let down the side window and breathed the cold night air deeply into his lungs. In some inexplicable way he was beginning to feel good about things. He turned to the Jamaican and said, 'What are you going to do now, Mac?'

Mac shrugged. 'That depends.'

'Depends on what?' Marlowe demanded.

'On how good an offer I get,' Mac retorted.

Marlowe smiled and shook his head. 'Don't run away with ideas like that,' he said. 'It's Maria's business now. She may have other notions.'

Mac shook his head and said definitely, 'That girl's got only one idea where you're concerned.'

Marlowe put a hand into his inside pocket and took out a sodden envelope that dripped water. He looked at it seriously and said, 'There's nearly two thousand quid in there, Mac. The way I look at it, Maria's entitled to a little compensation. A clever man could develop the business over the years and use this money without her ever realizing it.'

Mac grinned. 'Especially if he had the right kind of assistance.'

Marlowe clapped him on the shoulder. The truck swung into the farmyard, and as it moved forward the front door opened, flooding the porch with light.

She stood looking out from the step, her face in darkness. Marlowe wearily clambered down from the cab and turned towards her. He still couldn't see her face and as he took a hesitant step forward, she cried his name brokenly and ran towards him.

As he pulled her close in the prison of his arms, Marlowe was finally at peace. For the first time in his life he felt completely sure of himself and knew where he was going.

She turned and pulled him gently out of the darkness into the warm light of the house.

Jack Higgins
Cold Harbour £4.99

THE TIME: 1944

THE PLACE: CORNWALL

THE MISSION . . .

Cold Harbour

Craig Osbourne's war finished one dark night in 1944 when he was
pulled from the sea by the crew of a German E-boat – helpless, half
dead, frozen.

Until he found out who the Germans really were . . .

On the eve of D-Day, OSS was back in business – flying the flag of
the *Kriegsmarine*. Which explained why the Allies' deadliest killer
was sent straight back behind enemy lines, sporting the uniform of a
Colonel in the Waffen-SS.

It was a dirty, terrible war. And when you play dirty, you don't play
by the rules . . .

*'Higgins is violently back on form in favourite territory. Unbelievably
adventurous'* MAIL ON SUNDAY

Touch the Devil £4.99

'Touch the Devil and you can't let go' – an old Irish saying which
fits Frank Barry, 100-per-cent a terrorist; his ideology is money and
his track record is the best. When the Russians want review copies
of the latest NATO missile system, Barry's the man to deliver them.
The only man who can stop him is Martin Brosnan, poet and
scholar, a killer trained in Vietnam and polished in the service of the
IRA, currently a convict rotting in the French prison fortress of Belle
Isle. To get him out of there and working for British Intelligence is a job
for his oldest friend, Liam Devlin . . .

'Higgins . . . knows what he's about and does his job with skill, speed,
sang-froid' NEW YORK TIMES

The Savage Day £4.99

Simon Vaughan fought a dirty war in Korea, so the British Army eased him out. Ex-Major turned adventurer, firearms specialist with the best of Gun-running connections, and half-Irish as a bonus . . .

Now they offer to get him out of the Greek prison if he'll take on the IRA in Belfast . . .

'First class . . . packed with action, atmosphere and ingenuity'
BELFAST TELEGRAPH

'Among the greats of the high adventure storytellers'
EVENING NEWS

A Prayer for the Dying £4.99

'A thriller writer in a class of his own' FINANCIAL TIMES

Fallon was the best you could get with a gun in his hand. His track record went back a long and shady way.

This time the bidding came from Dandy Jack Meehan, an underworld baron with a thin varnish of respectability. Not exactly the type you'd want to meet in a dark alley.

The job Dandy Jack wanted doing was up North, but when Fallon got there he soon found himself changing sides.

Which put him in opposition to Meehan. A place where life expectancy suddenly gets very short indeed.

'100 per cent proof adventure' NEW YORK TIMES

Day of Judgment £4.99

1963: on the eve of Kennedy's historic visit to Berlin, Ulbricht's commissars plan their propaganda counter-strike from the red side of the Wall. Father Sean Conlin, survivor of Dachau an apostle of human freedom, is held captive in the impregnable fortress of Schloss Neustadt, his gaolers determined to make him admit to being a CIA hireling. The West must save Conlin, and a small band of intrepid men take on a rescue mission that could sway the course of history.

'Fast moving, meticulously organized, relentlessly demanding'
SUNDAY TIMES

Solo £4.99

'A brilliant but psychotic concert pianist who murders for pleasure in his spare time makes the mistake of killing the teenage daughter of a tough Northern Ireland SAS soldier, a trained and vicious killer himself. As soldier stalks maestro for vengeance, the tale builds to a tense, shattering climax' SUNDAY EXPRESS

Exocet £4.99

As the Argentine air force flew again and again against the Task Force, as the Harriers fought valiantly back, as push came to shove, the one missile that could take out a Type 42 destroyer ran low in the arsenals of Argentina. One man could get Galtieri the Exocets he needed. Two things might just get in the way. The KGB, always on the sidelines. And love, always waiting in the wings of war.

A Season in Hell £4.99

Spilled blood cries out for vengeance

When American socialite, Sarah Talbot learns that her stepson Eric has been murdered and his body used to smuggle heroin, she is determined that someone will pay. Sean Egan, ex SAS sergeant and a killer by instinct, is at first reluctant to act as assassin for her, until he discovers a personal stake.

Together they begin a desperate hunt for the ruthless man whose trade involves not only drugs but international terrorism. It is a search that plunges them into an unimaginable vortex of violence, but they both knew that –

the price for revenge is a season in hell

'Higgins uses almost every thrillerism in the canon, but with such shameless chutzpah that I enjoyed it all enormously . . . This time he has really excelled himself' THE TIMES

All Pan books are available at your local bookshop or newsagent, or can be ordered direct from the publisher. Indicate the number of copies required and fill in the form below.

Send to: Pan C. S. Dept
             Macmillan Distribution Ltd
             Houndmills Basingstoke RG21 2XS
or phone: 0256 29242, quoting title, author and Credit Card number.

Please enclose a remittance* to the value of the cover price plus: £1.00 for the first book plus 50p per copy for each additional book ordered.

*Payment may be made in sterling by UK personal cheque, postal order, sterling draft or international money order, made payable to Pan Books Ltd.

Alternatively by Barclaycard/Access/Amex/Diners

Card No.

Expiry Date

_____

Signature:

Applicable only in the UK and BFPO addresses

While every effort is made to keep prices low, it is sometimes necessary to increase prices at short notice. Pan Books reserve the right to show on covers and charge new retail prices which may differ from those advertised in the text or elsewhere.

NAME AND ADDRESS IN BLOCK LETTERS PLEASE:

....

Name_____

Address_____

_____

_____

_____

6/92